I0615264

Anna Brückner

Talks about English literature from the earliest times to the present day

present day

Three little plays

Anna Brückner

Talks about English literature from the earliest times to the present day
Three little plays

ISBN/EAN: 9783337206093

Printed in Europe, USA, Canada, Australia, Japan

Cover: Foto ©Andreas Hilbeck / pixelio.de

More available books at **www.hansebooks.com**

Vorwort.

Die Verfasserin des „Life in an English Boarding School"
(Velhagen & Klasing 1895) bietet in dem vorliegenden Werk-
chen eine Fortsetzung, die für die ersten Klassen und nament-
lich für Seminarabteilungen höherer Mädchenschulen bestimmt
ist. Sie will damit die Freude an der englischen Litteratur
wecken und stärken und das Verständnis der Entwicklung des
englischen Schrifttums in seinen Hauptvertretern und ihren
namhaftesten Werken in Poesie und Prosa erleichtern, ohne
jedoch den Lehrer entbehrlich machen zu wollen. Im Gegen-
teil. Auch dieses Buch setzt eine Lehrkraft voraus, die mit
Sprache und Dichtung, mit Verfassung und Lebensformen
Englands innig vertraut ist.

Die Verfasserin verkennt so wenig wie der Unterzeichnete,
dafs hierin eine gewisse Gefahr für das Buch liegen kann.
Eine flüchtige Durchsicht, die diesen Leitgedanken nicht ge-
nügend in Betracht zöge, könnte zu dem Urteil verleiten, als
halte sich die Darstellung vielfach an Äufserlichkeiten und Ein-
zelheiten. Diese Auffassung wäre unschwer zu widerlegen. Auf
Schritt und Tritt begegnet der Leser in den Unterhaltungen der
Mifs Stevens mit ihren Zöglingen dem Hinweis auf Werke, die
allgemein bekannt oder in der Schule schon gelesen und durch-
gearbeitet, auch wohl aufgeführt worden sind oder mit denen die
würdige Dame eine solche Behandlung beabsichtigt. Die Haupt-
arbeit also soll schon getan oder doch soweit gefördert sein,
dafs die Unterredungen, weit entfernt zu leeren Phrasen oder
zu Gedächtniskram zu führen, sich auf der sichern Grundlage
des Bekannten aufbaut oder zu weiteren Studien anregt. Das
Litteraturbuch will nur die Rundschau, den Rück- und Ausblick
leiten, wobei die einzelnen Werke vorher oder nebenher durch
Erzählen, Lesen, Besprechen, Vergleichen, Zusammenfassen,
zum Teil auch Auswendiglernen zum Eigentum der Schü-
lerinnen werden müssen. Das ist aber die einzige fruchtbare

und daher die einzige pädagogisch zulässige Art, Litteratur-
geschichte in der Schule zu treiben.

Schon die Gesprächsform deutet an, dafs die Verfasserin
kein trockenes Handbuch, keine Sammlung fertiger Urteile
liefern wollte. Wohl hat sie die besten Quellen*) gewissen-
haft berücksichtigt, aber sie hat sie durchaus selbständig
bearbeitet und dabei in Auswahl, Anordnung und Darstellung
des Stoffes ihr eigenes Urteil frisch und frei zur Geltung ge-
bracht. Ein solches Buch darf nur ein lebensvolles Buch sein
oder es darf nicht sein.

Beigegeben sind drei kleine Dramen: die beiden ersten
schliefsen sich an die englische Litteratur an, sofern das eine
den Sprichwörterschatz des englischen Volkes, das andere die
Behandlung englischer Litteratur in England selbst geistreich
veranschaulicht. Das dritte enthält einen von der Verfasserin
selbst in England erlebten Scherz, der ebenso wie die beiden
andern Stückchen auch zu Schulaufführungen geeignet und
willkommen sein dürfte.

Zugleich mag die dreifache Beigabe die Befugnis der Verfasserin erweisen, über englische Litteratur in englischer Sprache
zu schreiben, abgesehen von 15jähriger Lehrarbeit auf diesem
Gebiet, aus der die Schrift wie von selbst herausgewachsen
ist. Dafs das Manuscript zudem durch englische Fachleute
sorgfältig durchgeprüft worden ist, mag für ängstliche Gemüter
noch ausdrücklich betont sein. Ich selbst hege nicht den
mindesten Zweifel, dafs auch die "Talks about English Literature" dieselbe freundliche Aufnahme finden und diese ebenso
reichlich lohnen werden, wie das "Life in an English Boarding-School".

Freiburg im Breisgau, im Oktober 1898.

E. Keller.

*) 1. British Authors. (Nelson and Co.)
2. Collier's English Literature (Nelson and Co.)
3. Buckland's History of the English Literature (Cassell and Co.)
4. Stopford Brooke's Literature Primer (Macmillan and Co.)
5. Professor Dowden "Shakespeare" (Macmillan and Co.)
6. Seymour "Tales from Chaucer" (Nelson and Sons)
7. Lamb "Tales from Shakespeare" (Warne and Co.)
8. Professor Hales "Notes and Essays on Shakespeare" (George Bell and Sons)
9. XIX Century Prose (A. and C. Black)
10. XIX Century Poetry (A. and C. Black).

CONTENTS.

Talks about English Literature.

Division of Lessons.

Appendix: Three little Plays.

Berichtigungen und Verbesserungen.

S. 34, Z. 16 v. o.: Bei dem Worte parents mufs statt des Komma ein Apostroph stehen.

S. 56, Z. 15 v. u.: Lies neighbourhood statt neigbourhood.

S. 61, Z. 10 v. u.: Lies grown-up statt grown up.

S. 83, Z. 5 v. o.: Lies "Marmion" statt "Marminon".

S. 114, Z. 3 v. u.: Lies Then you will be a great "virtuoso" on the piano.

INTRODUCTION.

MISS STEVENS. I am glad to say your Senior Examination is over, but I think it is a great mistake that you had only the historical plays of Shakespeare to read to pass your local examination. I think well educated girls ought to be familiar with the whole history of English Literature.

JANET. I should so much like to know it; will you be so kind as to teach it us?

MISS STEVENS. I will give a manual of English Literature to each of you. You shall read up a chapter or a period every day, and the next day we shall talk about what you have read.

FRANCES. How very nice! In this way we shall peruse the chapter attentively.

EDITH. We began reading Collier's Literature at home — is it a good one?

MISS STEVENS. A very good Literature book indeed; you may keep it.

MARY. I should like to have a smaller book; there is so much to be remembered in Collier's.

MISS STEVENS. I will give you Stopford Brooke's Literature Primer.

MARY. Thank you very much; a Primer is just what I like.

MISS STEVENS. Janet, you shall have the "British Authors" — do you know it?

JANET. No, I don't.

MISS STEVENS. You will like it very much, there is a picture of each author.

JANET. Thank you so much, Miss Stevens.

MISS STEVENS. And to you, Frances, I will give Miss Buckland's History of English Literature, as you are so fond of books written by ladies.

FRANCES. You are very kind, Miss Stevens; that will be a very nice way of learning our Literature. I quite look forward to these repetitions.

MISS STEVENS. I am glad you do — if you do your part by reading attentively, you will have much to tell me.

I should like you to read leisurely as far as you can for to-morrow.

I will give you the books at once, if you will come downstairs to the library with me.

ALL FOUR. Thank you, we will — with much pleasure.

I. ANGLO-SAXON POETRY.

MISS STEVENS. Among every people the earliest form of literature is the Ballad.

Men emerging from savagery used to chant the story of their deeds in rough metre in order that the ring of the lines might help the memory to retain the tale.

The oldest existing specimens of British Literature are some scraps of Irish verse. You will have heard the name you little maiden of the "Emerald Isle".

FRANCES. "The Psalter of Cashel"; it was sung by the bards.

MISS STEVENS. It is ascribed to the fifth century, but very likely it was only compiled towards the end of the ninth century. There are only very scanty remains of Gaelic poetry, and they are of much later date than the earliest Irish ballads. Our "Scotch bonnie lassie" will know about them.

JANET. The Poems of Ossian. "Fingal" and "Temora", dating from the fourth century.

MISS STEVENS. They were published by James Macpherson in 1762 and 1763, and were very much admired by all contemporaries. Now they are generally looked on as literary forgeries. In Wales, which was the stronghold of Druidism, the profession of the bard was held in great honour. You can guess who was the hero of the bards. Mary?

MARY. The great Prince Arthur who was noted for his prowess against the Saxons. Is it true that he held his court at a Round Table, attended by his Twelve Knights?

MISS STEVENS. Legend has magnified his exploits. We learn a good deal about the Round Table in the Chronicle of Geoffrey of Monmouth. King Arthur was a favourite theme in the Middle Ages. A Norman Trouvère, Wace, sang his praises — as did Spenser in the "Faerie Queen", and Tennyson in the "Idylls of the King", as we shall hear later on. The old legend used to say that Arthur did not die, but is still alive, and ready to come forth whenever England needed him.

MARY. He seems to have been indeed the great favourite of the Middle Ages.

MISS STEVENS. So he was. There were besides these Celtic Writers also a few Latin authors, of whose works we will name those of the Irish missionary to the Gauls.

FRANCES. The Latin Poems of St. Columbanus.

MISS STEVENS. Thomas Moore, the Irish poet speaks of them as "shining out in this twilight period of Latin Literature with no ordinary distinction". The Anglo-Saxons brought their own poets with them from the Continent. Who sang "when the evening shadows fell and the mead bench was filled" to rouse the fiery spirit of the warriors or soothe their ruffled moods, Mary?

MARY. The Gleeman or Minstrel.

MISS STEVENS. The chief characteristic of the poetry of the Anglo-Saxons was a very regular alliteration, so arranged that, in every couplet, there should be two principal words in the first line beginning with the same letter, which letter must also be the initial of the first word on which the stress of the voice falls in the second line.

MARY. Is it like "Peter Piper picked a peck of pepper off a pewter plate" — and "Round the rugged rock the ragged rascals ran"?

MISS STEVENS. Just like that. — Which is their greatest epic poem, Edith?

1*

EDITH. "Beowulf", the hero of which is Beowulf, a Danish warrior, who slays the monster Grendel.

MISS STEVENS. The poetry of Beowulf is a striking picture of dim old Gothic days. As we read it, the gleaming of mail flashes in our eyes and we hear the clanging march of the warriors in Hrothgar's Hall, from whence Grendel had formerly carried off one "hearth-sharer" every night. — There is a second part of the "Saga"; who knows it?

JANET. Beowulf killed a fiery dragon who had wasted the land — he found in the dragon's cave a vast hoard of treasures. He was wounded by the dragon, and, as there was no cure for its poison, he left the treasure to his people, and bade them bury him on the high cliff by the sea-shore.

MISS STEVENS. Over his grave the warriors raised a mighty mound, and rode around it, singing a song of mourning for their chief. There is a manuscript of Beowulf, very much worn of course, in the British Museum in London.

II. CHRISTIAN POETRY.

MISS STEVENS. Yet the Teutons did not remain heathens. St. Augustine, sent by Pope Gregory, as you will remember, came over, and other missionaries also. They built religious houses (convents) in different parts of the country in order to be able to carry on their work. One of these houses had been built upon the Cliff of Whitby in Yorkshire. Do you know what poet lived there, Mary?

MARY. Caedmon, the first Christian poet in England. Is it true that Hilda, the pious Abbess of Whitby, taught him Christianity?

MISS STEVENS. He was one of Hilda's first converts. He had been quite an unlettered cow-herd or farmer. It was the custom of the time that, at each feast after supper, the harp was brought into the hall, and passed from guest to guest, every one being expected to sing some song in praise of the old Teutonic gods. Caedmon had listened to the wild songs extolling the deeds of Thor and Wodin, and he thought there was a far greater God than these heathen gods, whose praise he would like to sing. He used to slip out of the hall before it was his turn to sing. One night, he lay down to sleep in the stable and, in his sleep, a stranger came to him and said "Caedmon, sing me something". "I know nothing to sing" said the poor herd. "Sing the Creation" said the stranger, upon which, words of sweet music began to flow from the lips that had been sealed so long. Caedmon awoke, remembered the words of his "dream-song", and felt a new power in his breast.

JANET. What a wonderful inspiration this was! How very much surprised Hilda and the monks must have been.

MISS STEVENS. They wanted to test his new-found skill, and gave him a passage of the Bible to put into verse. So Caedmon spent the remainder of his life in composing his "Paraphrase" on the Creation and the Fall — on the History of Daniel and the Life of Christ.

MARY. I heard once that Milton copied from Caedmon; is that true?

MISS STEVENS. Milton cannot be accused of plagiarism; — he may have been inspired by that first true English poem. We may be proud that it is a Christian poem; that is much more important for us to consider.

The first English prose-writer was another monk of Northumbria; he was very learned, and spent his whole life in the same convent — at Wearmouth; he was born at Jarrow, on the banks of the Tyne. Tell me his name, Frances.

FRANCES. The Venerable Bede — he wrote the "History of the Anglo-Saxon Church". but he wrote in Latin, didn't he?

MISS STEVENS. His last work, a Translation of the Gospel of St. John, was written in English — it is the first effort to make English prose a literary language. You will know who is the next great scholar, the leading writer of Anglo-Saxon prose, Janet?

JANET. King Alfred the Great. He translated Bede's History of the Anglo-Saxon Church into Anglo-Saxon.

MISS STEVENS. He founded schools in the different parts of his kingdom. So that "every free-born youth, who has the means. shall attend to his book till he can read English writing perfectly". He even presided over a school in his own court.

MARY. Fancy King Alfred being a schoolmaster!

MISS STEVENS. He set a very good example to his people. He gave eight hours a day to the work of public affairs, viz. managing the business of his kingdom, eight hours to books and study, and he reserved only eight hours for sleep, meals, exercise and amusement.

MARY. No wonder great scholars from different parts of the world visited his court.

MISS STEVENS. King Alfred was anxious that his people should get interested in history. He not only translated the History of Orosius into English, but he made the Saxon Chronicle, which had chiefly been written by monks, and which had been only a dry record of events, a real History; — war-songs and battle-odes were quoted from it by his orders.

EDITH. How long was it continued after Alfred's death?

MISS STEVENS. It was continued down to the death of Stephen in 1154.

This period wich we have been talking about to-day is commonly called "the Anglo-Saxon or Old English Period". If you were to learn the language of this first period, it would almost be as hard to learn as any foreign language; but there is no need for you to learn it just yet — you may be learning other things for the present which are more useful to you.

III. ANGLO-NORMAN PERIOD, FROM WILLIAM THE CONQUEROR TO EDWARD III.

MISS STEVENS. The Norman Conquest wrought great changes on both the learning and the literature of England. William the Conqueror displaced many of the Saxon prelates who held sees at the time of the Conquest to make room for polished scholars from the Continent. Moreover he founded many fine abbeys and convents within whose quiet cells learned men could think and write in safe and honoured leisure.

Schools sprang up on every side. The great seminaries at Oxford and Cambridge, — already distinguished as schools in King Alfred's time, — were elevated to the rank of universities.

MARY. Which language was then used?

MISS STEVENS. The professional language of churchmen, by whom all learning was then monopolized, was Latin. There are several Latin writers — one of them who wrote the story of Arthur and his Knights we have already mentioned. Who remembers him?

JANET. Geoffrey of Monmouth.

MISS STEVENS. The Normans brought the Norman Romance with them; Chivalry was inseparable from it. The Romance relating to King Arthur and the Legend of the Saint Graal were mixed up in those days.

EDITH. Who else were celebrated in the Norman Romance?

MISS STEVENS. Alexander the Great, Charlemagne, and later on Coeur-de-Lion.

FRANCES. Isn't he said to have composed some songs himself?

MISS STEVENS. Yes, some military poems called "Serventois"; he had learned song-making from the Troubadours in Provence.

MARY. Were not these Norman Minstrels called by a Norman name?

MISS STEVENS. Jogler or Juggler from the Norman Jongleur. Those Yeomen Minstrels who were attached to noble houses wore the arms of their patron, hung round their necks by a silver chain. Many minstrels carried an instrument about; it is supposed to have been like a guitar and was called viele. The minstrel's dress bore some resemblance to that of the monks.

MARY. Did they use rhyme in their poetry?

MISS STEVENS. Yes, the Normans imported rhythmical verse from the Continent — a great improvement, although the number of syllables was often irregular still.

MARY. Was English quite out of fashion?

MISS STEVENS. It was left to the serfs and boors of the land, as they could not understand the new language; yet the poets clung to English, as we see in the first book written after the Norman Conquest. Who knows the title of it?

JANET. It is a translation by a Somersetshire priest Layamon or Loweman from a French poem: "The Brut."

MISS STEVENS. Brutus, the fabled son of Aeneas, was said to be the founder of the British nation and, although "The Brut" is a translation from a French poem, there are not fifty French words in the whole of it. An Augustine monk called Orm or Ormin wrote a poem; he called it after his own name. You will know the title now, Edith?

EDITH. The "Ormulum".

MISS STEVENS. It is a poem of nearly twenty thousand short lines, without rhyme of any kind, but with a regular number of accents — however there are not five French words in the whole poem. Orm was extremely particular about his spelling; when an accent struck a consonant after a short vowel, he insisted on doubling the consonant.

MARY. But what is the subject of the "Ormulum"?

MISS STEVENS. It is a metrical paraphrase of the service of each day with the addition of a sermon in verse. "Transition English", in which these poems are composed reached its goal in the realm of poetry, in an allegorical work written by a west-countryman, a monk, a man of the people, of intensely radical sympathies. What was its title, Edith?

EDITH. "The Vision of Piers the Ploughman" written by William Langland about the year 1362.

MISS STEVENS. The principal object of the author seems to have been to chastise the priests of the time for the wicked way in which they lived. It became the book of those who desired social and church reform. It was eagerly read by the free labourers and serfs who collected round Wat Tyler, the rebel, for it was written in the old English manner, so that the very ploughboy could understand it. Its fame was so great that it produced imitators.

MARY. Please tell me what this vision is about?

MISS STEVENS. It is difficult to say in a few words. The author fancies himself wandering over the Malvern Hills; he lies down on the grass and falls asleep. He dreams that he sees spread out before him "a fair field full of folk". —

This field represents the world; in the far east rises the Tower of Truth and in the dim west "Death dwelt in a deep dale". Then a struggle ensues between Truth and Falsehood, the former represented as a "comely maiden", the latter as a blear-eyed "babber-lipped" old wretch. The dreamer finds that, "Than Truth and True Love is no Treasure better"; but on awaking he remembers that the world he is living in is far from loving Truth, so that the victory he had dreamed of is not real and he begins to weep bitterly. — As I said, this poem wrought so strongly on men's minds that its influence was almost as wide spread as Wiclif's great work. What do you know about him, Frances?

FRANCES. John Wiclif was born in 1324, in Yorkshire. In 1361, he became Master of Balliol College, Oxford. He began to preach against the wicked practices of the begging friars and against the corrupt doctrines of the clergy. In 1377, he was appointed Rector of Lutterworth in Leicestershire — he was often charged with heresy, but John of Gaunt supported him, and he published the first Translation of the Bible into English. Wiclif died in 1384.

MISS STEVENS. The Translation of the Gospels alone can be identified as the work of Wiclif. This translation had much influence on fixing our language; he made the English tongue the popular language of religious thought and feeling. Wiclif has been called "the Father of English Prose".

IV. GEOFFREY CHAUCER.

MISS STEVENS. As William Langland represents the part of the nation that spoke pure English, so Geoffrey Chaucer represents that part which spoke English with a large mixture of Norman-French.

JANET. Did the people understand that?

MISS STEVENS. It had become quite familiar to the middle class through the work of Friars who "interlarded" all their speech with French words in their intercourse with the craft of merchantmen. Medicine and all the science of the time were in their hands. By the time Edward III began to reign, the Normans and Saxons had become completely intermixed; the old hatreds were gone; the conquered and the conquerors had united to conquer foreign foes. Chaucer's poems, though saturated with Norman-French, are so much like the English which we speak to-day, that we can understand a great deal without any explanation. This is why he is called "the Father of English Poetry".

But you are anxious to tell me about his life, Mary.

MARY. Geoffrey Chaucer was born in London; many dates are ascribed to his birth, ranging from 1328 to 1340. His father was most likely a wealthy wine-merchant in Cheapside. He sent his son to a grand school. He seems to have been fond of reading the old poetical romances, but just as fond of strolling (roving) in the fields round London in the month of May.

MISS STEVENS. I see you are thinking of the pretty lines on the Daisy that are quoted in most readings books.

MARY. Yes, I am; they run thus:

"Of all the flow'rës in the mead
Then love I most these flow'rës white and red.
Such as men callen daisies in our town.
To them I have so great affection,
As I said erst, when comen is the May,
That in my bed there daweth me no day,
But I am up and walking in the mead,
To see this flow'r against the sunnë spread."

MISS STEVENS. We are not sure whether Chaucer was educated at Oxford or at Cambridge, nor do we know in what way the young poet won the favour of John of Gaunt, who introduced him at Court. Will you please go on with Chaucer's biography, Edith?

EDITH. When Prince Lionel went to France with the English army in 1359, Chaucer went with him; he had the misfortune to be taken prisoner, but he turned the months of his captivity to good account by reading the romances of the Troubadours and Trouvères. He was ransomed by the

King at the Peace of Bretigny in 1360. It was at Court that Chaucer became acquainted with Philippa de Rouet, a young lady-in-waiting on Queen Philippa. He loved this young lady and he wrote a poem for her, called "the Dream". After his marriage with Philippa, he and his wife were engaged in the household of John of Gaunt.

MISS STEVENS. In 1369 the Duchess Blanche, the wife of John of Gaunt, died, and Chaucer wrote a poem of mourning for his royal friend whose sorrow was great.

Chaucer was a great favourite with the old King too, because he was not only a poet and a scholar, but also because he was a clever and useful man of business. You know where the King sent him to, Frances?

FRANCES. In 1372 Edward III sent him to Italy to try and arrange with the Duke of Genoa for the choice of some port in England, to which goods might be sent from Italy for sale to English merchants.

MISS STEVENS. This visit to Italy was no doubt for Chaucer the realisation of one of the brightest dreams of his life, and it certainly left on his mind a vivid impression, which could not fade away, for Italy was at that time the very home of literature, and especially of poetry. Do you know the names of the three great Italian poets who lived about that time?

JANET. Dante, Petrarch, and Boccaccio.

MISS STEVENS. Dante had died about 50 years before; his great Allegorical poem "La Divina Commedia" was generally admired and read. Petrarch and Boccaccio were still living; Chaucer may have seen both poets. Petrarch may have read some of his Sonnets to him, and Boccaccio may have told him stories from the "Decamerone".

MARY. This is a collection of a hundred tales, which seven ladies and three gentlemen — who had fled to a quiet country-house at the time of the plague in Florence — tell each other in order to pass the time.

MISS STEVENS. Chaucer learned a great deal abroad which he could never have learned at home, for foreign books were rare in England at that time, when each copy had to be written with pen and ink. This Italian influence is seen in the choice of subjects for his later poems, of which we shall speak presently... Tell us about his return to his native land, Janet.

JANET. In acknowledgment of the success of his mission to Italy, the King granted Chaucer "a pitcher of wine daily", and afterwards, instead of it, a payment of twenty marks a year. Chaucer obtained a lease for life of a dwelling-house at Aldgate too, and he was appointed Comptroller of Customs.

MARY. What a very prosaic occupation for a King's Poet or Laureate! —

MISS STEVENS. The poet was only obliged to keep the books and fill in the bills of lading with his own hand; he was allowed to engage some one to attend to the other duties, so that he had leisure to write poetry. Which two poems did he write next?

FRANCES. "The House of Fame" — a dream in which the poet sees a crowd of persons pressing into the "House of Fame" seeking fame, and "the Legend of good Women", of which I remember: "Goodë women, maidens and wives, that are true in love all their lives!"

MISS STEVENS. During the latter part of Edward the Third's reign, and in the early part of that of Richard II, John of Gaunt was in great power and able to do much for his poet brother-in-law, for the Duke of Lancaster had married Catherine Swynford, the sister of Philippa Chaucer; but at length a change came. The misrule of King Richard caused a Commission of Regency to be appointed, and in 1387 one of the first acts of the commission was to take from Chaucer his pension and his appointment. At the same time his wife died. The next ten years of his life were a constant struggle with poverty.

MARY. He was now old too, poor man!

MISS STEVENS. It was during these very years that he set to work upon his best and greatest poem "The Canterbury Tales", of which we will speak presently. The poet did not live to complete his work. He died in 1400. After Henry the Fourth's accession, he received a large pension again, so that he was well off. We are told that Chaucer never uttered one word of grumbling or bitter feeling at his reverse of fortune; he bore it manfully and with a Christian spirit. His body was laid to rest in Westminster Abbey.

V. THE CANTERBURY TALES.

MISS STEVENS. Now we come at last to the "Canterbury Tales" of which you learned part of the Prologue, telling us where the pilgrims met "in Aprille with his showrës swootë". Who remembers these lines?

JANET. I do.

"Byfel that, in that seasone on a day,
In Southwark at the Tabard as I lay,
Redy to wenden on my pilgrimage
To Canterbury with ful devout courage,
At night was come into that hostelrie
Wel nyne and twenty in compainye.
Of sondry folk, by aventure i-fallë!
Ir felaweschipe, and pilgrims were they allë.
That toward Canterbury wolden rydë,
The chambers and the stables weren wydë,
And wel we weren esed attë beste."

MISS STEVENS. The "nyne and twenty" pilgrims were of all sorts and conditions of men, as you know — namely, Mary?

MARY. A Clerk of Oxford, a jolly Monk, the Franklin, the Knight, the Squire, a wife of Bath, a Priores-, the Pardoner, the Pedlar, a Yeoman, a Merchant. a Doctor of Physic, and so on.

MISS STEVENS. In imitation of Boccaccio's "Decamerone", Chaucer made them each tell a tale "to beguile the time" as the road was bad and long. — Which story do you know best, Frances, as you read them all in Mary Seymour's "Tales of Chaucer"?

FRANCES. The nicest, I think, "the Knight's Tale". Two close friends have been taken prisoners by Duke Theseus of Athens. Looking forth from their prison window one day, they behold the lovely Emily. sister of the Duke's wife, walking in the garden. Both princes are immediately smitten with her beauty, and the friends, now rivals for the hand of the same lady, become hateful to each other. In course of time, the one, Prince Arcite, is released, the other, Palamo, contrives to escape. They meet by accident in a grove, and are fighting like wild beasts when Duke Theseus comes suddenly upon them. At first the Duke feels inclined to put the princes to death, but finding out the cause of the quarrel, he commands that they shall meet and fight together at a tournament, and the one who shall gain it is to win Emily as his prize. Arcite is proclaimed the victor. — Unfortunately, however, while he is riding along the lists, he is thrown from his horse, and soon lies dying at the feet of his beloved Emily. He has to tell her to take Palamo as her husband, and he speaks in his old friend's praise with the kindness of a true knight. Death creeps up his limbs, and his breath fails him,

"But on his lady yet he cast his eye,
His lastë word was 'Mercy Emelye'".

MARY. What a very touching story! May I tell the "Clerk's Tale"?

MISS STEVENS. If you like, but tell it briefly.

MARY. In Italy, or rather in Lombardy, there lived a Marquis called Walter. He was exceedingly dear to his people because of his wise and gentle government; but he had his faults too — he had a great love of pleasure. The devoted people thought if their lord were married, he would be less frivolous — so they sent "a certain number of chosen" to go up to the castle to ask his leave to choose a good wife for him. The noble Marquis thanked the spokesman and his companions for their kind offer, but said that if he was to give up the liberty he enjoyed so much, it was only fair that he should choose his wife himself, and so he did.

At a very short distance from the Castle, in a small and humble village, there lived in a miserable hut a poor maiden. Griselda. Young as she was, she had a brave heart and was always peaceful and happy under the pressure of work or of want. Lord Walter's thoughts turned to Griselda, as he had often heard of her virtue, industry, and love to her old father Janicula. He ordered everything to be prepared for his wedding, and then he went to Janicula to ask permission to marry his daughter. The old man trembling from head to foot, answered: "That which my Lord wishes, let it be." Then Griselda was consulted. She was obliged to promise "to be obedient in everything, whether she was treated well or ill".

She humbly answered: "If such is your wish, my lord, I consent to be your wife, and I will swear never to disobey or resist your wishes."

So Griselda was "arrayed in beautiful garments", and became a marchioness. The first year of her married life passed smoothly. Griselda was very much beloved by the people, as she remained modest. A little daughter was born to her, and now her troubles began.

The Marquis wishing to try his wife's stock of patience, ordered her to give up her little baby daughter to be exposed to starvation as she could not be the heiress. The unhappy mother only said "My will is yours, my lord", as she had once promised when the Marquis sought her in her poor abode.

Several years passed by, and then the much desired son was born — but again the cruel father had this child taken away from the low-born mother, and again she did not utter one word of complaint.

The Marquis tried his wife still harder; he sent her back to her low cottage and told her that he wished to marry a "highborn lady". Griselda went back apparently quite content. Now the Marquis was convinced of his wife's virtue, and great was the joy when Griselda and the people were told, that "the highborn lady was no other than herself, that the little daughter, who had grown into a fine young lady, was hers, and the young baron who came with her to court was her son, who had been brought up by the Duchess of Bologna, the Marquis' sister. Isn't it a nice tale in honour of woman's virtue?

MISS STEVENS. Indeed it is. Chaucer thought very highly of woman's virtue.

VI. CONTINUATION.

MISS STEVENS. There is another Tale somewhat like the one we heard. Who can tell it me?

JANET. "The Man of Law's Tale." — Once upon a time there dwelt in Syria a company of rich traders, who dealt in fine cloth, silks and spices. One year they made a journey to Rome to sell these goods. Just then men were speaking much about Constance, the daughter of the Roman Emperor, for she was not only most beautiful, but also most virtuous. The merchants were very anxious to see this fair lady, and they succeeded in doing so. When they returned, they were so full of the praise of Dame Constance that the Sultan became anxious to gain her for his bride. He sent messengers to Rome to woo the Emperor's daughter. Constance did not like to marry a pagan prince, but it was arranged by the mediation of the Pope that the Sultan and his lords should receive baptism before Constance went there to be married. The treacherous mother of the Sultan was displeased with her son's faithlessness to Mahomet's law; she devised a scheme to prevent the introduction of Christianity into her country. She received Constance very kindly, and told her son she would take care of her whilst he prepared for the wedding. While the Sultan was away, his mother's servants took Constance to a ship which had no rudder or compass, placed some food and clothing in it, and bade her get back to Italy as best she could. The poor affrighted maiden appealed to Heaven to preserve her from being drowned, and her prayers were answered; the little boat was driven to the Northumbrian coast. The keeper of an old castle on the shore took the poor shipwrecked maiden to his wife who soon loved her dearly, for Constance did not disclose her rank, but made herself very useful by working like a servant. There were three other Christians in Northumbria, and soon the keeper and his wife Hermengilde became converts too. A bad knight fell in love with Constance, but as she would not love him in return, he killed Hermengilde and put the blood-stained knife by the side of the unconscious Constance and stole away. The good King Ella came to the keeper's house to find out the perpetrator of the crime; he was soon convinced of Constance's innocence, and ordered the knight to be slain. Soon afterwards he made Constance his dear wife, but her mother-in-law, Donegilde, hated her because the King had become a Christian for her sake.

When Ella was away in Scotland, a little son was born to him. A messenger was despatched to Scotland, but Donegilde managed to change the King's message, and ordered that Constance and her little son should be put back on the vessel which had once brought her to Northumbria. She was again pushed off to sea with her baby; clothing and food sufficient for a long voyage were put into the boat. The unfortunate mother looked up to Heaven again, and she was not forsaken. The Roman Emperor had sent an army to Syria to avenge his poor daughter's fate; and as the army was returning home victoriously, one of the senators encountered the vessel which contained the poor mother and her child. Neither threats nor entreaties could draw from her any acknowledgment of her station, so she was taken by this kind lord to his home, and treated very kindly; although the senator's wife was Constance's aunt, she did not recognise her, as she was so much changed by her many sorrows.

When Ella came back to Northumbria, and learned what had happened, he became so furious that he slew Donegilde in his rage. After a while, he began to grieve for destroying his wicked mother, and as a penance for his sins he undertook a pilgrimage to Rome. You may easily guess what happened. He found his long lost wife in a marvellous way. The Emperor, who had grown old now, was more than delighted to see that his dear daughter was still living, and that he had a little grandson. He settled that the little son, Maurice, should succeed him and remain with him to be educated at Rome. Ella and Constance went back to Northumbria, and lived happily and peacefully ever after, doing much good in their home, and setting the people a good example, so that they all became Christians.

MISS STEVENS. You have not told us this Tale very briefly, but very well indeed, thank you.

Now, Edith must tell us a Tale, a short one, lest we feel tired out. (worn out, exhausted.)

EDITH. I don't think you will, for I meant to tell you the very amusing Tale of the "Nuns' Priest":

There was once a poor widow who dwelt with her daughters in a small cottage, and was content with humble fare. In her little yard, the widow had a few fowls, one of which, a cock named Chanticleer, had not his equal in crowing — he was a fine fellow too. The fairest of all his seven hens was Dame Partlet, she was Chanticleer's favourite and always sat next to him on the perch when they went to roost. One night Chanticleer made such dismal noises in his sleep, that Dame Partlet grew quite alarmed. "What ails you?" she said to him. "O dear dame," answered Chanticleer. "I have had a terrible dream; it seemed to me that a horrible beast was walking about in our own yard. His body was black and his eyes were bright and fierce. I felt very much afraid of him —" "Don't be a coward!", Dame Partlet replied, "else I shall be ashamed of you. A wise man, Cato, once said: "Never pay heed to dreams". Chanticleer was not quite convinced of the truth of Cato's saying — he told the good Dame that he had heard that many dreams had been fulfilled. By that time morning had dawned, and Chanticleer flew from the perch, and called his seven hens to follow him. He led them outside the yard to look for some grains of corn, little dreaming that a cunning fox lay concealed there, waiting his opportunity to fall on Chanticleer. It so befell that the cock espied a butterfly on the leaves of the plants amid which the fox was lurking, and approaching nearer, he saw the intruder. He was going to fly away, when the fox addressed him in sweet words: "Gentle friend," he said, "I have come to hear you sing, not to do you any harm. I heard you had a voice like an angel." Chanticleer was so charmed with this fine speech that he began to stretch his neck and to crow with delight.

Now the fox sprang from his hiding-place, caught him up, and carried him off to his hole in the wood.

The seven hens made an awful noise, when they saw their defender borne away; the widow and her daughter heard them, and, starting up, reached their cottage-door just in time to see the fox darting off in the direction of the wood.

They took (seized) some sticks and staves and began to chase the fox; all the men and women who heard them cry, joined them, and even all the animals ran with them; there was never more confusion in the world than these shrieking people and animals made running after the fox. Yet they would never have been able to save the poor cock's life, if a sudden thought had not prompted him to say to the fox: "Sir, were I you, I should speak to these noisy churls and say: "A pestilence fall on you. I will devour this cock in spite of all your efforts." And the fox was so stupid as to open his mouth to speak, and Chanticleer was so intelligent as to free himself with one quick movement, and to fly on to a tree overhead. "Good friend," said the fox, "come down again. I have done you great wrong to drag you here; come down and I will explain all." "No, no," said Chanticleer "you have beguiled me once with your fine speech — I'll never be deceived again by smooth words."

MARY. Let us hope he never was disturbed by bad dreams either, poor Chanticleer!

MISS STEVENS. This Tale has been useful to several fabulists; it teaches such a good lesson, which many people will never learn, but which I trust you will ever remember, viz.

Not to be deceived by fine dress or by fine speech. and never to judge by outward appearance, but rather to look "for the hidden treasures." —

This has been a very long lesson, but a very interesting one.

VII. ELIZABETHAN LITERATURE.

MISS STEVENS. In the fifteenth century, the interest in classical literature grew owing to the Revival of Letters. A great many nobles became lovers of books. It was only after the religious and political disturbances at the end of Henry the Eighth's reign, when England was at peace and prosperous again, that poetry revived as an art. In this reign Sir Thomas More wrote "Utopia", and two noblemen travelled in

Italy and brought back to England the inspiration they had gained there. Who were they, Janet?

JANET. Sir James Wyatt and the Earl of Surrey.

MISS STEVENS. The language of their poetry though Italian in sentiment, is more English than Chaucer's, that is, they use fewer Romance words. They handed down this purity of English to the Elizabethan poets who were, however, far from imitating foreign poetry; for with the general awakening of national life under Queen Elizabeth new veins of thought were opened, the love of stories grew, and the old English ballads and tales were eagerly read and collected. With whom did the glory of the new literature arise, Janet?

JANET. With Edmund Spenser, who was born in London in 1553. While at Cambridge, he got intimate with Sir Philip Sidney.

MISS STEVENS. Do you remember who Sir Philip Sidney was, Mary?

MARY. Indeed I do. Elizabeth at first called him "the jewel of her dominions". and long refused to listen to his ardent wish to go to war; but then Sidney fell into disgrace; he retired from court. and wrote his famous book "Arcadia". In 1586 he went to the Low Countries and fought in the battle of Zutphen, where he received a deadly wound. When he was carried past a wounded soldier. he turned the cooling draught from his own parched lips to slake the dying thirst of this poor fellow-sufferer. He was only 32 years old when he died.

JANET. Sir Philip Sidney introduced Spenser to the Earl of Leicester, the Queen's favourite, who introduced him at court. The result of royal favour was a grant of land in Ireland, the estates of Kilcolman in the county of Cork, of which his other friend Raleigh had already received a large share.

MARY. What illustrious friends Raleigh had! Did he get these acres of Irish land to reward him for throwing his cloak on the muddy ground when Her Gracious Majesty Queen Elizabeth passed?

MISS STEVENS. He was knighted as he served with almost incredible bravery in Ireland during the rebellion of the Earl of Desmond, from whom these lands were taken; he was not only a brave soldier, but also a brave sailor. In the reign of James the First, he was charged with high treason, and put into the Tower, where he wrote his "History of the World".

MARY. Was he beheaded?

MISS STEVENS. Yes, he was executed although he did not plead guilty; but let me tell you of his visits to his friend in Ireland. Spenser's Castle of Kilcolman stood near a beautiful lake in the middle of an extensive plain, girdled with mountain ranges. Soft woodlands and savage hills, shadowy river-glades and rolling ploughland were all there to gladden the friends' hearts. Near the wooded banks of the gentle Mulla which ran by the Castle, Spenser composed "the Faerie Queene" and read it to his brilliant friend.

And Raleigh was so delighted with the beautiful poetry that he urged the poet to cross the sea with his precious "cantos", as he called them, to lay them at the feet of the Queen. Now go on, Edith.

EDITH. Elizabeth honoured them with her approval, and rewarded the genius and the flattery of Spenser by granting him a pension of £ 50. After having published "the simple song", as Spenser modestly called his first three books, he went back to Ireland, where he held a responsible position as Sheriff of Cork. Soon after his marriage with a lady named Elizabeth. he published his second three books. In 1596 he crossed to England again, and published the fourth, fifth and sixth books of his great work. Scarcely had he settled in his bright home again when a rebellion broke out, the insurgents attacked Kilcolman Castle so suddenly and so furiously that Spenser and his wife had to flee for their lives from the blazing ruin, leaving behind them their youngest child who was burnt to death.

FRANCES. You see Spenser did not try to be friendly with the wild natives; he followed the opposite policy of keeping them down with an iron hand.

EDITH. Broken-hearted and almost in poverty, the poet died in London three months later, in 1598. He was buried in Westminster Abbey, near Chaucer.

VIII. THE FAERIE QUEEN.

MISS STEVENS. Spenser wrote some minor poems — the "Shepheardes Calendar", a pastoral poem or eclogue; "Mother Hubbard's Tale", a satire on the intrigues of court life, and others; but we will only speak of his chief poem of which you learned part of the Opening Stanzas. Who will repeat them?

MARY. I will, please.

A gentle Knight was pricking on the plaine,
Ycladd in mightie arms and silver shielde,
Wherein old dints of deep wounds did remaine,
The cruel markes of many a bloody fielde;
Yet arms till that time did he never wield;
His angry steede did chide his foming bitt,
As much disdayning to the curbe to yield:
Full jolly knight he seemed and faire did sitt
As one for knightly giust and fierce encounters fitt.

And on his breast a bloodie crosse he bore,
The dear remembrance of his dying Lord,
For whose sweete sake that glorious badge he wore,
And dead, as living ever, him ador'd:
Upon his shield the like was also scor'd,
For soveraine hope, which in his helpe he had.
Right, faithful, true he was in deede and world;
But of his cheere did seeme too solemn sad;
Yet nothing did he dread, but ever was ydrad.

MISS STEVENS. Will you please tell us in prose now what adventure the Red-Cross Knight who represents the militant Christian was bound upon, Frances?

FRANCES. He wanted to achieve a glorious deed which Gloriana, "the Queen of Faerie land" gave him to do, viz "to prove his puissance upon a Dragon, horrible and stearne". In spite of the plots of the wizard Archimago, or Hypocrisy and the wiles of the witch Duessa, or Falsehood he slays the dragon that ravaged the kingdom of Una's, or Truth's father, and thus wins the hand of that fair princess.

MISS STEVENS. Janet, you might mention the heroes of the other adventures.

JANET. Sir Guyon, or Temperance, is the hero of the second adventure, — Britomartis, or Chastity — a Lady-Knight — of the third; Cambel and Friamond, typifying Friendship, of the fourth; Artegall, or Justice, of the fifth, Sir Calidore, or Courtesy, of the sixth.

MISS STEVENS. The poet only finished six books of this allegorical poem. He intended to write twelve. Prince Arthur, who is chosen as the hero of the poem, falls in love with the Faerie Queen, and, armed by Merlin, sets out to seek her in Faerie Land. She is supposed to hold her annual feast for twelve days, during which twelve adventures are achieved by twelve knights. The poet attempted to interweave with his bright allegories the history of his own day. Gloriana, the "Faerie Queen", represents Queen Bess whose red wig becomes in his melodious verse "yellow locks, crisped liked golden wire".

MARY. What outrageous flattery!

MISS STEVENS. You must not be so shocked. It was the fashion of the day; poets are only human. Artegall, or Justice, is Lord Grey of Wilton; Duessa, Envy, or Falsehood is poor Mary Stuart.

JANET. What a shame! I never knew that, else I should not have perused the poem with such delight.

MISS STEVENS. The stanza in which the great poem is written bears the poet's name. How many lines are there, Frances?

FRANCES. There are nine.

MISS STEVENS. It is the Italian ottava rima with a ninth line, an Alexandrine, which the poet added to close the cadence. Modern poets have proved the power of this grand Spenserian stanza. Spenser wrote capital prose as well as exquisite verse. He wrote a "View of the State of Ireland", a dialogue in which that land and the habits of its natives are finely described.

IX. THE ENGLISH DRAMA.

MISS STEVENS. Before we begin with our illustrious dramatist, we must speak of the Drama, as we have not yet spoken about it. At the time of Queen Elizabeth, the habit of play-writing became common. At every ceremonial, whenever the Queen visited one of the great lords or a university, a masque or a play or a pageant was acted

MARY. In "Kenilworth", the Earl of Leicester engages a troup of actors to play before her; — it must have been a great expense to the lords, must it not?

MISS STEVENS. An enormous expense, as they rivalled each other. Let us hear first of the Origin of the Drama, Frances.

FRANCES. The Drama began with the Miracle-Play which represented some portion of Scripture history or some incident of the life of some saint.

MISS STEVENS. Who were the first actors, Edith?

EDITH. The clergy, because the Miracle Plays were first represented in the churches. In 1268 the town-guilds began to take them into their own hands.

MISS STEVENS. Two new kinds of plays were written. Which were they, Frances?

FRANCES. The Mysteries, representing a mysterious subject, such as the Resurrection — and the Moralities in which some moral principle was established, such as virtue triumphing over vice.

MISS STEVENS. We have still three sets of such plays — the Towneley. Chester and Coventry plays.

MARY. Who collected them?

MISS STEVENS. The town-guilds most likely — from the towns they went to the houses of the nobles and to the court. To enliven these plays, historical characters were introduced — Brutus represented patriotism — Aristides, Justice, and so on. But soon a demand arose for plays which should picture human life. Who knows the name of the first English comedy, by Nicholas Udall, master of Eton?

MARY. I know. It is "Ralph Royster Doyster"; it was first acted by the Eton boys.

MISS STEVENS. It is a picture of London life and manners at that time. The plot is the story of a self-conceited, vainglorious young man, and the consequent ridicule and loss of respect which he draws upon himself. There is plenty of fun, such as boys would enter into. Who knows when the first English tragedy was written?

MARY. I do again. It was in 1561 that the first English tragedy was written by two members of the Inner Temple. Latin plays had been acted by the law-students of the Inns of Court as well as by the students of the universities. It is called "Ferrex and Porrex" or "Gorboduc".

MISS STEVENS. The plot of the play is the strife going on in the family of King Gorboduc who divided his realm in his life-time between his sons, Ferrex and Porrex. The sons fell into dissension. The younger killed the elder. The mother who had loved the elder more dearly, out of revenge killed the younger. The people, moved by the cruelty of the act, rose, and killed both father and mother. The nobility, enraged at the rebellion of the people, destroyed the rebels. then fell afterwards to civil war among themselves as to the accession to the crown. In this war, they and their children were slain, and the land remained for a long time almost desolate and miserably wasted.

MARY. Dear me, this is a tragedy worse than "Hamlet"; no one survives to tell the sad tale of their death!

MISS STEVENS. The authors, Sackville and Norton, intended to put the evils of disunion very strongly forward, in order that all might understand and take the lesson to heart. They founded the plot on a bloody story of ancient British history. It is written in regular blank verse, and consists of 5 acts between which there is always a chorus as in the Greek plays.

JANET. Where was this tragedy first acted?

MISS STEVENS. At the Inner Temple at the Christmas festivities, and a fortnight after it was acted in Whitehall before Queen Elizabeth and her court.

EDITH. It seems funny that the law-students of the Inns of Court should act before the Queen.

MISS STEVENS. As I told you, before "Ferrex and Porrex" there were only translations of Greek and Latin plays, but as soon as other English plays besides this one were written, great nobles had their servants and retainers taught to act. In 1574, the Earl of Leicester obtained a patent for his servants, giving them permission to act within the city of London and in any town in England.

FRANCES. Where did they act, please?

MISS STEVENS. The place usually chosen for the performance was an inn-yard. In 1576 the Earl of Leicester's company built the Blackfriars Theatre in which Shakespeare acted. This was the greatest dramatist of that and all other times, and he gives the crowning glory to the Elizabethan Literature.

X. PREDECESSORS OF SHAKESPEARE.

MISS STEVENS. Shakespeare had several clever predecessors, Who knows their names?

FRANCES. Lyly, Peale, Green and Marlowe.

MISS STEVENS. Lyly is the author of "Euphues", a book of travels full of endless metaphors from the classics and natural history. In six years the two parts of "Euphues" ran through five editions. so great was its popularity. It became the fashion to talk "Euphuism". Peele and Greene make their characters act on, and draw out one another in the several scenes; but they have no power of making a plot. Peele wrote historical dramas; Greene, plays of home-life. Marlowe rose by degrees into mastery of his art. What are the names of his plays, Edith?

EDITH. The "Jew of Malta" — "Edward II" and "Doctor Faustus".

MISS STEVENS. The first depicts the passions of greed and hatred; we find these vices again in one of Shakespeare's characters.

MARY. In Shylock, who loves his jewels more than his daughter.

MISS STEVENS. "Edward II" or rather "The Troublesome Raigne and Lamentable Death of Edward II" shows us the misery of weakness and the agony of a king's ruin. You all know, who "Doctor Faustus" was?

EDITH. He was a German magician who sought knowledge to gratify his own pride.

In his eager pursuit of knowledge, he employed the aid of evil spirits and sold his soul to Satan.

MISS STEVENS. Marlowe worked these stories into a powerful drama, in which the contest between good and evil, between temptation and conscience is set forth with great earnestness and energy.

You see each of Marlowe's plays illustrates one ruling passion in its growth, its powers and its extremes. Marlowe's verse is "mighty"; he may be said to have improved the verse of the drama, blank-verse, and also to have created English tragic drama. Do you know anything of his life, Frances?

FRANCES. Marlowe led a wild and irregular life like all the play writers and actors of his time. He was killed in a brawl in a London tavern in 1593, when he was only 30 years old.

XI. WILLIAM SHAKESPEARE.

MISS STEVENS. When Marlowe died, Shakespeare was just beginning to write original plays. Tell us all you know of the life of William Shakespeare before he came to London. Janet.

JANET. William Shakespeare was born in 1564, probably on the 23rd of April, St. George's Day, as he was baptised on April 26th, at Stratford-on-Avon in Warwickshire. His father, John Shakespeare, was a comfortable burgher who dealt in wool, leather, skin, gloves and hosiery, in Henley Street. He is said too to have owned some land near Stratford, belonging to his wife Mary Arden, who was born a lady and an heiress to boot. At one time Master Shakespeare ranked so high among the burgesses of Stratford that he sat on the bench as High Bailiff or Mayor of the town. The poet was born during this prosperous time, and he was sent to the Free Grammar School of his native town, where, however, he learned only "little Latin and less Greek", as his friend Ben Jonson tells us.

MISS STEVENS. The beds of violets and banks of wild thyme, the beautiful woodland scenery amid which the boy grew up, may have induced him often to neglect his daily tasks and to wander along the gently flowing Avon with a fishing-rod in his hand.

Stratford-on-Avon was at the junction of two old Roman roads and the highway between Oxford and Birmingham, so that the poet had the other great advantage of getting passing glimpses of the outside world. It is very likely too that his parents took the lad to see the pageants at Kenilworth in 1577, and, moreover, "strolling players" often came to Stratford and put up at the famous Bear-Tavern; they initiated young William at an early age in the drama of that period. Please, go on, Frances.

FRANCES. The fortunes of the Shakespeare household declined, and this is probably the reason, why William left school at thirteen altogether. We do not know to which occupation he took. He is supposed to have been usher in a school, or clerk in a notary's office, because he is so well acquainted with law-terms. He was still just as fond of strolling about in the country as when he was a boy; there is a story that the wild youth often saw the moon rise over the dark oakwoods of Charlecote Park, while he lurked in the shadow, waiting for the deer as a poacher.

MISS STEVENS. Sir Thomas Lucy of Charlecote Park was one of the land-owners who employed a large staff of keepers to retain his deer within the bounds of his own property, for whenever they strayed they became fair game for whoever could shoot them. Lively youths in hot pursuit of a stag would find it hard to pause at the limit where it ceased to be lawful to hunt one; and deer-stealing became a fashionable sport much affected by Oxford students. The ready sale for venison to London tavern-keepers would increase the zest of more needy poachers. The tradition has been for many years firmly fixed in Warwickshire minds that William Shakespeare was brought before Sir Thomas Lucy, Justice of the Peace, and severely fined or locked up, perhaps both, for stealing his deer. Do you know what the boyish poet is said to have done in revenge, Mary?

MARY. He wrote some doggerel rhymes, and stuck them on Sir Thomas' park gate. Rather daring of him! The knight's rage grew so violent that Shakespeare had to flee from Stratford.

MISS STEVENS. Modern authorities discard these traditions with scorn. However, strange to say, Shakespeare made Sir Thomas ridiculous as Shallow in the "Merry Wives of Windsor"; the only instance of Shakespeare's using for material his own personal adventures. There was another reason why he left Stratford.

JANET. At the age of nineteen, he had married Anne Hathaway, a yeoman's daughter of Shottery, a beautiful hamlet one mile distant from Stratford. She was more than eight years older than himself. He did not get on with his wife who was not well educated.

MISS STEVENS. It is more probable that it was the need of providing daily bread for his wife who indeed was not of such "noble lineage" as the Shakespeares and the Ardens, and for his children, Hammet, Susanna and Judith, and, perhaps also for his parents who had become very poor, that caused Shakespeare to go up to London in 1586. What was his first employment in London, Edith?

EDITH. We do not exactly know. According to one tradition he held horses at the theatre door, as many spectators came on horseback to the play-house; another tells us that Shakespeare's first occupation was that of call-boy or prompter's assistant in a theatre where three Warwickshire men, one a native of his own town, held a prominent position. Before long we hear of his taking small parts himself.

MISS STEVENS. However Shakespeare may have earned his first shillings in London, it is certain that, unlike the other actors of his time, he soon became prosperous and even wealthy. In 1568 he already held a share in Blackfriars Theatre, having previously by his acting, and by the adaptation of old plays and the production of new ones, proved himself worthy to be much more than a mere sleeping-partner in the concern. He became also part-owner of another theatre.

FRANCES. The Globe Theatre. Was Shakespeare a good actor, Miss Stevens?

MISS STEVENS. He never rose to distinction as a player, but he was honoured with the special notice of his Queen, and he lived among the fine London folks, and associated every day with the noblest and richest Englishmen of that brilliant time. This was quite a distinction for an actor, as his fellow-actors were held in very low esteem.

JANET. Why were they so much looked down upon?

MISS STEVENS. Their lives justified the prejudice. As you heard of Marlowe, they often fought and quarrelled after having spent the night in revelling. Shakespeare was quite an exception — he had early learned what poverty meant, and knew that it rested with himself to repair the broken fortunes of his family. Every year he went back to Stratford by coach or on foot. He enjoyed walking along the quiet country-roads, and most likely he generally stopped at Oxford for a night's rest. His company journeyed about too. As his fame brightened, his purse filled; and the great poet was soon able to buy an estate, New-Place, "for the rest and solace of waning life". When did he finally retire to Stratford, Janet?

JANET. In 1612. He spent the three last years of his life "in ease, retirement and the conversation of his friends". New-Place was famed for its hospitality. His great friend, Ben Jonson, visited him in March 1616, and some say the undue festivity on that occasion was the cause of a fever from which the great poet died on April 23rd of that year.

MISS STEVENS. It is much more probable that the disease was contracted from the notorious amount of filth in the streets, for in those days drainage was not at all understood and sewers had never been heard of at Stratford-on-Avon. So many years of incessant nervous labour must have told upon the poet mentally and physically, but at 52 he was perhaps only too ready "to shuffle off this mortal coil", as he says in "Hamlet". By his own wish, the great dramatist was buried at Trinity Church, Stratford. It is supposed that he himself wrote the lines placed upon his tomb:

"Good friend, for Jesus' sake forbeare
To dig the dust enclosed here:
Blessed be the man that spares these stones,
And curst be he that moves my bones."

MARY. Please, Miss Stevens, was Shakespeare reconciled to his wife?

MISS STEVENS. We may hope he was. In the making of his will, that precious document now in the British Museum, Shakespeare showed that sane forethought which characterized all his transactions, and his affairs were in good order. Both his daughters were married; his son had died in 1596. Shakespeare left to his wife his second best bed, rather a strange bequest. Susanna was the inheritor of the bulk of the property, she kept up the hospitable repute of the house, and in 1643 entertained Queen Henrietta Maria for three days in a style befitting her position.

XII. SHAKESPEARE'S PLAYS OF THE FIRST PERIOD.

MISS STEVENS. Many biographers divide Shakespeare's career of authorship into Four Periods. It is probable that before leaving Stratford he had sketched a part at least of his "Venus and Adonis", as it is full of country sights and sounds. When it was published in 1591—93 he became at once the favourite of men like Lord Southampton. Before he became famous he had "touched up" old plays. The first he is usually thought to have retouched is "Titus Andronicus" and, some time after, the First Part of "Henry VI". His first original play was "Love's Labour's Lost", in which he quizzed and excelled the Euphuists in wit. It was followed by the involved and rapid farce "The Comedy of Errors". Who knows why it is so called?

MARY. Twin brothers, Antipholus by name who had been separated by a shipwreck, are so much like each other, that their own servants who are also twins and had been brought up with them, do not know "which is which". The wife of one even mistakes one for the other, — in the end all is explained by the father who had gone from Syracuse to Ephesus in search of his children.

MISS STEVENS. Out of these frolics of intellect and action Shakespeare passed into pure poetry in the "Midsummer Night's Dream", in which he shows his wonderful power of imagination. Tell us the Dream, Edith.

EDITH. Two true lovers, Hermia and Lysander, were going to flee from Athens to be married secretly, as Hermia's father had chosen a certain Demetrius for his daughter's husband. Demetrius had formerly made professions of love to Hermia's friend Helena, who became very jealous now. Hermia confided the secret of her elopement (flight) to Helena, little thinking she would reveal it to Demetrius.

When night came, Hermia went out into the wood to meet Lysander; this wood was the favourite haunt of Oberon and Titania, the fairy king and queen. Unfortunately "the royal pair" were always quarrelling, "so that their attendant elves would creep into the flower-bells and acorn cups trembling with fear." Just then Oberon wished to have a little changeling boy for his page whom Titania had stolen from his nurse, but Titania refused to give him up, so Oberon resolved to avenge himself by teasing her.

MISS STEVENS. You might tell us in what way he accomplished this purpose. Janet.

JANET. He summoned his favourite, Puck, who was a very mischievous sprite, and bade him seek a certain little flower called "love in idleness", the juice of which, sprinkled on the eyelids of those who slept would make them love the first thing they beheld on awaking. Whilst Oberon was thinking how he would squeeze some drops of his marvellous juice on Titania's eyelids to get the boy from her he saw Demetrius coming into the wood in search of Lysander and Hermia. Helena followed him, reminding him how dearly he had once loved her. Oberon felt sorry for this despised

maiden, and, when Puck returned with the flower, he resolved
to make her happy once more. He bid Puck find Demetrius
and, if he was sleeping, drop the juice on his closed lids,
that on awaking he might see Helena and feel his love for her
return. However, Puck first crept up to the little queen, and
pressing the flower on her eyelids, said:

"What thou seest when thou dost wake,
Do it for thy true-love take."

In another part of the wood, Hermia was resting while
Lysander kept guard over her. After a while, sleep fell on
him. Puck, fancying he must be the cold lover, applied the
little purple flower to his closed eyes. Unfortunately Lysander's glance on awaking first fell on Helena, who had wan-
dered that way and all his love went out to her. When
Hermia awoke, she found her lover gone. Oberon, seeing
the mistake, hid himself, and touched the eyes of Demetrius
with the wonderful juice and, when he awoke, he beheld
Helena followed by Lysander, speaking loudly of his love for
her. When Demetrius also began singing her praises, Helena
thought it some jest, and bitterly reproached Hermia for it.
Hermia declared that she was rather badly treated by all.
When finally Lysander and Demetrius went apart to fight with
each other for the love of Helena, Oberon overhung the night
with a thick fog and bade Puck drop the juice of another
flower upon Lysander's eyes by which he should be made to
forget Helena and love Hermia as before, and thus each lady
should be happy and think that all which had occurred was
but some evil dream. Then Oberon went in search of Titania
who was still sleeping; seeing a foolish clown, Bottom, close
by, he put the head of an ass on his shoulders for mischief's
sake. When the fairy queen opened her eyes, she called the
clown with the ass's head beautiful, and talked to him as if
she loved him. Oberon, finding her thus, made her promise
him the little boy he had so long coveted for a page.

MISS STEVENS. This comedy is bright with the poetry of
a young man's fancy, which throws a tender grace over all
the insignificant duties of life — typified by the little work of
the fairies "hanging dew drop in the cowslips" and "killing
cankers in the musk-rosebuds". At that time, everybody

believed in elves and fairies. There are three distinct stories: a love-story, a fairy story, and a farce, bound together to make an harmonious whole. Probably the play was written in honour of the marriage of a noble friend, Southampton or Essex. Italian story then laid its charm upon the poet.

"The Two Gentlemen of Verona" preceded the southern glow of passion in "Romeo and Juliet".

MARY. We read the story of the unhappy lovers of the house of Montagu and Capulet in Lamb's Tales, and we often quoted "Oh Romeo, Romeo, why art thou Romeo"!

EDITH. And I remember with horror that it was the sad quarrels of these two hostile families that drove the young lovers to commit the desperate deed.

FRANCES. And I think Friar Laurence ought to have advised them better. He was wrong in wedding Romeo and Juliet without their parents, consent and above all in giving Juliet the sleeping-draught.

MISS STEVENS. You had better allow competent people to judge this tragedy of Shakespeare, in which he first reached tragic power. It is a young man's work, in which Youth and Love are brought face to face with hatred and death. "The course of true love never runs smooth". Another love-play belongs to this early period. Which is it, Janet?

JANET. "All's Well That Ends Well." Helena, a physician's daughter, is married to Bertram, the Count of Roussillon by the order of the king, whose life Helena had saved. Bertram leaves his bride, and Helena wins his love after a long time of trial and suffering.

MISS STEVENS. The patriotic feeling of England now seized upon the poet, and he turned from love to begin his great series of historical plays with "Richard II" and the first part of "Henry VI", then later on "Richard III" and "King John", of which you acted Act IV Scene I last Saturday evening.

MARY. I pity Prince Arthur's mother, Lady Constance, the wife of Geoffrey, very much too. Philipp of France was very horrid when he told her she was as fond of cherishing her grief as she had been fond of cherishing her son.

EDITH. I like the last lines of the play:

"This England never did nor never shall
Lie at the proud foot of the Conqueror.
Come the three corners of the world in arms,
And we shall shock them; naught shall make as rue
If England to herself do rest but true."

MISS STEVENS. I will add that Shakespeare treated history according to the dramatic purpose he had in view. The last lines you quoted, Edith, would be followed by the uproarious applause of the audience, as "King John" was produced in 1595, only 7 years after the defeat of the Armada, and all Englishmen were proud of their victory. This historical play completes Shakespeare's first Period, which Professor Dowden names "In the workshop".

XIII. PLAYS OF THE SECOND PERIOD.

MISS STEVENS. The Second Period which has been named by the same author "In the world", opens with the "Merchant of Venice". You know it very well as you have read it. It was written in 1597, as we know by some later "Sonnets" which the poet wrote then. He was in a sad mood at that time, he had "gained his experience and the experience had made him sad". This is the key-note to the Merchant's character; he "holds the world, but as the world — a stage where every man must play a part and mine a sad one". Nevertheless he is a staunch friend to his kinsman Bassanio, the fine young scholar.

EDITH. I can't forgive Bassanio for forgetting his dear friend after having won "fair Portia's hand".

MISS STEVENS. He never doubted that Antonio would be able to pay the debt as "His fortune was not in one bottom trusted". He was not superficial, else he would not have chosen the lead casket saying: "So may the outward things be least themselves. The world is still deceived with ornament." What do you think of Portia, Janet?

JANET. I like her immensely — she is not only "fair, and fairer than that word", but she is an obedient daughter

3*

too — she respects her dead father's will, and she is highly intellectual when she pleads Antonio's cause.

MISS STEVENS. That passage on "the Quality of Mercy" is one of the finest poems in our language. As to Shylock we must pity him, "for sufferance was the badge of the whole tribe".

Pure comedy followed in the "Taming of the Shrew" and in the three comedies of Falstaff; which are they, Frances?

FRANCES. The first and second parts of "Henry IV" and the "Merry Wives of Windsor".

MISS STEVENS. The latter play is an offshoot from the two former. A tradition reports that it was written by the order of the Queen who was so well pleased with that admirable character of Falstaff in the two parts of "Henry IV", that she commanded the poet to continue it for one play more to show Falstaff in love.

MARY. Queen Elizabeth's taste differed greatly from that of one of my maiden aunts, who declares Falstaff awfully vulgar.

MISS STEVENS. Maiden ears were accustomed to coarse language in those days. English literature knows no humorous creation to be set beside Falstaff; we all admit, however, the necessity of the utter banishment of Sir John from the Prince, when Henry enters upon the grave responsibilities of kingship.

To which play am I alluding, Janet?

JANET. To my favourite one, "Henry V", a splendid dramatic song to the glory of England.

MISS STEVENS. Again Shakespeare turned to write of Love, not to touch its deeper passion as before, but to play with it in all its lighter phases in "Much Ado about Nothing", and another comedy, "where the time fleets carelessly"; who has read it?

FRANCES. I have: "As You Like it." Rosalind and her dear friend Celia fled to the forest of Arden and became shepherdesses, and their lovers Orlando and Oliver went out in search of them, and of course they succeeded in finding the young ladies (the two maidens) in spite of their disguise; and the play ends with the double wedding.

MISS STEVENS. "Twelfth Night" is the last play of this period, during which Shakespeare's life had changed and his mind with it. His best friends fell into ruin: Essex perished on the scaffold, Southampton went to the Tower, Pembroke was banished from Court.

He passed from comedy to write of the sterner side of life, to tell the tragedy of mankind. This he does in his third Period, called "Out of the depth", by Professor Dowden.

XIV. SHAKESPEARE'S PLAY OF THE THIRD PERIOD.

MISS STEVENS. The third Period opens with "Julius Caesar" in 1601. We may have scattered through the narrative of the great Roman's fate, the expression of Shakespeare's sorrow for the ruin of Essex. You all learned Mark Antony's Oration in Act II, Scene I.

JANET. How well Shakespeare shows the fickleness of the mob in this play!

MISS STEVENS. The action of this tragedy is very slow, but the characters are well delineated. Brutus is ruled by intellectual doctrines and moral ideas; he leads a most noble, high and stainless life, but his public action is a series of practical mistakes. What does Antony exclaim, when he finds the lifeless body of Brutus?

JANET. "This was the noblest Roman of them all:
His life was gentle, and the elements
So mixed in him, that nature might stand up
And say to all the world:
"This was a man!"

MISS STEVENS. Portia, Cato's daughter, his wife, is equal to, and worthy of him.

"Hamlet" followed, for the poet felt like the Prince of Denmark, that "the time was out of joint".

FRANCES. We read the story of Hamlet by Mary Seymour — and we repeated the beautiful Soliloquy "To be or not to be, that is the question". Why is Hamlet so slow to act?

MISS STEVENS. Hamlet is disqualified for action like a Teuton by his excess of the reflective tendency and by his unstable will. As he is naturally sensitive, he receives a painful shock from the hasty second marriage of his mother; the springs of faith and joy in his nature are thus already embittered, when the terrible discovery of his father's murder follows with the injunction laid upon him to revenge the crime. Upon this again follow the repulses which he receives from Ophelia.

JANET. I pity Ophelia. I don't admire her like Portia; but why does Hamlet pretend to be mad?

MISS STEVENS. He is aware that he is surrounded by spies; except for one loyal friend, Horatio, he is alone among enemies. He assumes the part of one whose wits have gone astray; partly to baffle them, partly to create a veil behind which to seclude his true self, partly because his moral nature is indeed deeply disordered.

MARY. Does he think Ophelia faithless too? That is rather strange of him!

MISS STEVENS. He regards Ophelia as no more loyal or honest to him than his mother had been to her dead husband.

FRANCES. The King is quick to act, when he sees that Hamlet is his foe.

MISS STEVENS. Hamlet does not delay acting at the last moment either: he displays a terrible power of sudden and desperate action then. It was only "the fear of something after death", that had made him so slow before. His character forms a striking contrast to that of the king, whose conscience does not "make him a coward". —

Hamlet was followed by the tragicomedy "Measure for Measure" and the three great tragedies "Othello", "Macbeth" and "King Lear".

You know the story of "Othello", "that loved not wisely, but too well", so well, that we may talk about the characters at once.

MARY. How could the beautiful and gentle Desdemona marry a Moor?

MISS STEVENS. Othello was of a free and noble nature and could tell "the tale of his love in a very winning way". He was naturally trustful with a kind of grand innocence, but he retained some of his barbaric simpleness of soul in the midst of the subtle and astute politicians of Venice.

FRANCES. That Iago was a hellish villain. Are there any other base characters like him in Shakespeare?

MISS STEVENS. There is no character so full of serpentine poison and power as Iago. He is envious of Cassio, who is of a chivalrous nature, and possessed by enthusiastic admiration of his great general and his sweet wife.

Let us speak of "Macbeth" now. Our Scotch girl will know this tragedy well.

MARY. What cruel people these Scotch are. Don't get angry, Janet. But that constant shedding of blood reminds one of the "Tales of a Grandfather", where one Scotch noble murders the other.

MISS STEVENS. There is indeed much bloodshed in Scottish History, but, on the other hand, we find a great many heroic actions too.

Macbeth possessed elements of honour and loyalty in his nature. He causes the gradual ruin through yielding to evil within and evil without. He has physical courage, but moral weakness; he would have the gains of the crime without its pains. But when once his hands are dyed in blood, he hardly cares to draw back and the same fears which had tended to hold him back from murder, now urge him on to wholesale slaughter. At last the gallant soldier fights for his life with a wild and brutelike force. What do you think of his wife?

FRANCES. Lady Macbeth is stronger-minded than her husband. The ruling passion in her nature is ambition. Having once fixed her eyes upon an end, the attainment of the meek Duncan's crown, she accepts the inevitable means, and nerves herself for the terrible night's work.

EDITH. In the end, however, her own strength gives way. I wonder why Macbeth does not feel more sorry for his wife's death.

MISS STEVENS. You see he had sunk too far into the apathy of joyless crime to feel her loss deeply. Husband and wife form another contrast.

MARY. Please, Miss Stevens, may we act Lady Macbeth walking in her sleep on Saturday next? I should like to take the part of the Ladyship, who cannot rub out "the spot, the damned spot".

MISS STEVENS. If you like, your sister may be the gentlewoman and Frances the doctor.

Let us speak now of "King Lear", the most touching of Shakespeare's tragedies.

You must understand that Lear is supposed to have lived 800 years before Christ.

JANET. But I can't understand why the old father acted so foolishly as "to divest himself of rule, territory and state".

MARY. And I can't understand why he didn't know his daughters better.

MISS STEVENS. Lear is the greatest sufferer in Shakespeare's plays, partly through his own fault. Goneril says of him: "The best and soundest of his time hath been but rash", so, before the infirmities of age came, he was most impatient. He expires in an agony of grief, after having been delivered from his passionate wilfulness.

EDITH. What his grief must have been when he cursed his daughter, saying: "How sharper than a serpent's tooth it is to have a thankless child!" and when he called out on the heath in the awful stormy night:

"Spit, fire! Spout, rain!

Nor rain, wind, thunder, fire are my daughters.

I tax not you, you elements, with unkindness;

I never gave you kingdom, called you children."

MARY. What a contrast the pure loving tender-hearted Cordelia forms to her sisters.

MISS STEVENS. Goodness and evil are clearly severed from each other in this play. Goneril is the more formidable, Regan acts under her bad influence; they both get worse as the play proceeds. What do you think of Kent?

FRANCES. I admire his pure loyalty after the bad treatment he had received. But why is there a jester in the play?

MISS STEVENS. The court fool is entirely out of place. However, the poet wanted the jester to lighten the plot, to relieve the tragic strain with an air of comedy. Moreover

the fool alone can gain Lear's ear and tell him how foolishly
he had acted. Besides the jester proves to us, how much
Cordelia was beloved, for he pined away "since his young
mistress went to France".

To this third Period also belong "Troilus and Cressida",
"Antony and Cleopatra", "Coriolanus" and "Timon of Athens".

XV. SHAKESPEARE'S PLAYS OF THE FOURTH PERIOD.

MISS STEVENS. The fourth Period proves to us that
Shakespeare had risen above sin, sorrow and fate into peaceful
victory; that's why Professor Dowden calls it "On the heights".
Like his great contemporary, Bacon, he left the world and his
own evil time behind him and, with the same quiet dignity, sought
the stillness of country life. It may be that he showed his
little grandson "the bank where the wild thyme blows, where
oxslip and the nodding violet grows", which he had delighted
to see himself in his youth. The country breathes through
the dramas of this fourth Period. Which are they, Frances?

FRANCES. The "Winter's Tale", "Cymbeline" and the
"Tempest".

MARY. Isn't it in the "Winters Tale" that Paulina shows
the wonderful statue of Hermione to Leontes?

MISS STEVENS. Yes it is — and how glad the king was
when he saw that it moved.

JANET. Leontes was fearfully jealous; he didn't deserve
to be forgiven by his poor wife and his beautiful daughter
Perdita, whom he had ordered to be exposed in infancy.

MISS STEVENS. We shall see that in the poet's last plays
forgiveness and reconciliation are the common ending.

JANET. Yes it is true; in "Cymbeline", Imogen endures very much too.

MISS STEVENS. Remember in life that "The silence of pure
innocence persuades, when speaking fails".

MARY. Dear me, it must be hard to be silent when you
are wronged!

MISS STEVENS. We will now hear the story of Shakespeare's last play, as we heard that of his first. Please begin, Edith.

EDITH. The "Tempest" opens with a violent storm at sea, in which we see a ship in extreme danger. On board are Alonzo, King of Naples, Ferdinand, his son, Sebastian, his brother, Antonio, Duke of Milan, Gonzalo, an old counsellor and other lords and servants. They are returning from Tunis, where they have been to the marriage of the King's daughter. The ship is drifted towards the shore of an unknown island. Suddenly it strikes upon a rock and breaks into pieces. This storm had been raised by spirits under the command of a magician, Prospero, who with his daughter Miranda lives on this enchanted island. During the storm Prospero relates to his daughter for the first time that he had once been Duke of Milan, but as he was quite taken up with his studies he had left the management of his dukedom to his brother Antonio. Antonio made an agreement with the King of Naples that he would become his vassal, if he helped him to take possession of the duchy.

Prospero was seized and placed with his little two year old daughter upon a rotten boat; his books and clothes were put into the boat which drove to this rocky island. Here he could gratify his own tastes. He found spirits on this lonely island, who were ready to do his bidding at a word.

Among the spirits there is one called Ariel, whose ideal of life is to live merrily "among the blossoms in perpetual summer". He can "come with a thought" and he has power over the winds too. It was he who raised the awful storm.

MISS STEVENS. Will you please continue, Frances.

FRANCES. Ariel gets Ferdinand separated from the rest of the passengers and crew, and leads him by magic song towards Prospero's cave. Miranda is at once touched by pity for him, and Ferdinand is struck with her beauty. Prospero tests the love of Ferdinand; he commands him to carry heavy logs of wood and to pile them up before the cave ere the sun sets. Ferdinand patiently bears Prospero's hard words, and cheerfully accomplishes the heavy task for Miranda's sake, as he sincerely loves her. In the meantime the other passengers in the ship are dispersed in two groups. The first consists of the King of Naples, his brother Sebastian, the usurping Duke of Milan, Antonio, Prospero's brother, Gonzalo, and other courtiers. As they wander through the island and the King is mourning for Ferdinand as dead, a plot is laid by Sebastian and Antonio to kill the King, while he is asleep. But Ariel wakes the sleeping king and sets before "the three men of sin" the wrong which had been done to Prospero. Now the thought of their misdeeds presses heavily upon them — the other group is composed of the king's butler, his jester and Caliban, a monster who does all the menial work for Prospero. These plot to kill Prospero and take possession of the island. Ariel tells Prospero of all that has happened, and Prospero tells him to bring the king and his party to his cave. He receives them in his old dress as Duke of Milan. The reconciliation takes place between the brothers, and it is arranged that Ferdinand shall marry Miranda. It turns out that the ship has been put in complete order and is ready for sea. Prospero abjures his magic, releases Ariel, and henceforth he will live as Duke of Milan and rule wisely.

MISS STEVENS. As I said, the final triumph of good over evil is put forward again in this play. It is rich in the wisdom and toleration that good men gain in later life, but dramatically it is not one of the greatest plays. It contains beautiful poetry, but a stage production is extremely difficult. — Shakespeare still wrote part of "Henry VIII" in honour of the marriage of Princess Elizabeth. (Febr. 1612 or 1613). Fletcher, of whom we shall speak by and by, expanded the play into a historical masque or show-play.

We have now spoken of the best-known of Shakespeare's plays; they are so many-sided that we may read them over and over again and we shall still find them as fresh as ever. There is always, as we have seen, a bright story fascinating to a child; there is the true picture of life; there is the lesson of moral truth to guide us in our actions. And on the surface of the play lie the neat little sayings in which great truths are so compactly wrapped up that we can use them as house-hold words.

XVI. THE STAGE IN SHAKESPEARE'S TIME.

MISS STEVENS. I think we ought to speak of the stage in Shakespeare's time to-day. The stage was generally quite simple, as the play-house had been an inn-yard before; the centre of the building was open to the sky and without seats, only the stage and the gallery were roofed; admission to the open space or yard was very cheap, from one penny to sixpence, while as much as a shilling or half a crown was given to obtain a place in the best parts of the house.

JANET. These seats were on the rush-strewn stage, were they not?

MISS STEVENS. Yes they were; young gallants sat there; they drank, smoked and joked, while they were waiting for the black-robed Prologue.

EDITH. Where did the ladies sit?

MISS STEVENS. If ladies appeared in the room or boxes, it was considered correct they should conceal their faces and wear masks.

MARY. How very funny! I wonder they cared to go; they must have felt uncomfortable. Did Queen Elizabeth put on a mask too?

MISS STEVENS. When she went to the play-house, and she did so very often, as she liked Shakespeare's plays, no other audience was admitted.

MARY. I remember reading an anecdote, that she once dropped her pocket-handkerchief on the stage and that the ready-witted Shakespeare, who was acting some king, stooped saying "But ere this be done, let us pick up our royal sister's handkerchief".

FRANCES. Where did the poor people sit?

MISS STEVENS. They did not sit, they stood in the pit; they behaved very badly before the performance began, cracking nuts and fighting for bitten apples.

EDITH. When did the performance take place?

MISS STEVENS. It generally began at three o'clock and lasted from two to three hours.

MARY. But how did they know when it would begin?

MISS STEVENS. A flourish of trumpets announced that the play was going to begin, and a flag was hung out from the top of the building. Upon the third sounding, the prologue was delivered, the curtain divided and drawn back, and the actors were discovered.

EDITH. How were they dressed?

MISS STEVENS. They appeared in costumes which were often costly, but which made slight pretensions to historical propriety.

JANET. What a pity — as the costume in accordance with the time gives one such a good idea of it. How did they indicate a change of scenery?

MISS STEVENS. They put a suggestive piece of stage furniture — a bed to signify a bed-chamber, a table with pens upon it to signify a counting-house, or often they put only a board bearing in large letters the name of the place of action. There was no movable scenery then such as there is nowadays.

EDITH. How was the scenery hung?

MISS STEVENS. With arras, and overhead there was a blue canopy representing "the Heavens". When a tragedy was to be acted the stage hangings were black.

JANET. Was there only one storey?

MISS STEVENS. At the back of the stage there was a balcony which served many purposes — it was the inner room, upper-room, window, balcony, battlement, hill-side, Mount Olympia, any place in fact which was supposed to be separated from, and above, the scene of the main action.

FRANCES. I see — on this balcony Juliet appeared to Romeo, and the play in Hamlet was acted.

MISS STEVENS. Just so — that reminds me of the advice Hamlet gives to the players; he warns them against the fashionable abuse of that time, to amuse the audience with extempore joking.

MARY. I think this joking of the clown most amusing. I do like Launcelot in the "Merchant of Venice".

MISS STEVENS. So do I — but in other plays the clown is rather uncouth. Shakespeare himself disliked the traditional

mode of providing sport for the occupants of the yard or pit.
Between the acts there was dancing and singing too.

Finally the actors knelt, and offered up a prayer for the
Queen.

FRANCES. Who acted the female parts?

MISS STEVENS. Boys or young men with unbroken voices.
It is thought that Shakespeare himself often did. It was only
after the Restoration that women actors came on the stage;
that was French influence very likely.

FRANCES. We English seem to have copied foreigners in
many ways; did they ever copy us?

MISS STEVENS. To be sure, child; Shakespeare, for instance, has been copied and translated by French and German poets.

MARY. Goodness me, what do the French understand
about Shakespeare? I should like to know.

MISS STEVENS. You are right. I only said they copied
him: Voltaire understood him so little that he called him "un
sauvage ivre", but the Germans helped us to see the beauty
of our greatest poet — their mind is more congenial to ours
— they even look upon Shakespeare as their own, as they
have excellent translations. You will be surprised to hear
that Shakespeare was not appreciated in England as he deserved it till about a century later.

The Drama fell into decay after his death. Beaumont
and Fletcher, as well as Massinger, Ford and Webster were
blind supporters of James I's invention of the divine right
of kings; besides they are "studiously indecent". In contrast to
them, Shakespeare is "as white as snow". His friend, "Rare
Ben Jonson" strove with manliness and courage to lead
men to live for more serious aims in the times of the Stuarts,
when the stage became quite degraded. Do you know the
names of his best-known plays?

FRANCES. "Every Man in his Humour" and "Every Man
out of his Humour".

MISS STEVENS. The first was a comedy, the second a
satire, directed against the follies of London life.

XVII. JOHN MILTON.

MISS STEVENS. The tone of Society changed with the accession of the Stuarts. The strife in politics began. England ceased to be one.

Unfortunately our greatest religious poet Milton was involved in this strife. Let us hear his biography, Janet.

JANET. John Milton was born on December 9th 1608 in London. When the boy was twelve years old, he was sent to St. Paul's School. He wrote his first poem, the hymn

"Let us with a gladsome mind
Praise the Lord, for He is kind"

before he was fifteen years old. His father who had been disinherited for adopting the Protestant faith, was very fond of music, and Milton inherited his father's taste.

The boy was very studious, and so his father sent him to Cambridge in 1624. On account of his delicate beauty he was called "the Lady of Christ's". (College.)

MARY. I don't wonder they jeered at him, because his hair was parted in the middle as all his pictures show.

MISS STEVENS. They might have spared their mockery. for "the blonde beauty" was even then showing signs of wondrous genius in its dawn. In 1629 he composed his magnificent "Ode on the Morning of Christ's Nativity". Where did he go to after having taken his degree, Frances?

FRANCES. He spent five delightful years in his father's country house at Horton in Buckinghamshire, enjoying nature and turning over Latin and Greek authors.

MISS STEVENS. His first poems "l'Allegro" (Mirth) and "Il Penseroso" (Melancholy), "Comus", and "Lycidas" round which the scent of the hawthorn hedge is ever fresh, reflect his calm and quiet life. "Comus", a masque to the glory of temperance was once acted by the Choral Society here. It is a beautiful allegorical play. "Lycidas" is a poem in memory of a dear college friend who was drowned. Let us go on with his biography, Edith.

EDITH. When Milton's mother died, the sweet charm that bound him to Horton was broken and in 1638 he went to Italy. He visited the blind Galileo at Florence, then he went to Rome. His imagination was kindled by Italian scenery, sculpture and music.

MISS STEVENS. While the poet was in Italy, the thought of writing an epic poem on the subject of King Arthur, appears to have become a fixed purpose in his mind. But what did he do, Mary, when at Naples he heard the sad news of the Civil War?

MARY. He returned to England "inasmuch as he thought it base to be travelling for amusement, while his fellow-countrymen were fighting for liberty". At the meeting of the Long Parliament, we find him in a house in Aldersgate Street, which his father had taken for him, teaching his nephews and some other boarders. In 1643 he was married to the daughter of a Royalist.

MISS STEVENS. This marriage was a hasty and not a happy one. Mary Powell went home to her father's house after a few weeks, as she preferred the merriment in her father's home to the quiet life in Milton's house. The poet was very sorry, and thought that a divorce would be better as his wife refused to return. He even wrote some pamphlets on that subject. However, his wife was glad enough to return to him, when her father's affairs were on the verge of ruin. Meantime he had written his great political pamphlet. What is it called, Janet?

JANET. "Areopagitica": A Speech to the Parliament for the Liberty of unlicensed Printing".

MARY. I see he compared Parliament to the Areopagus in Athens.

MISS STEVENS. In it Milton pleads that Truth may not have its mouth stopped by a Committee, many of whom fail to recognise its voice. He then wrote a famous letter "On Education" of which the main doctrine, that of filling the mind with a knowledge of Latin and Greek is not accepted in the present day. On the death of his father, the poet was fairly well provided for, and removed to a smaller house near Lincoln's Inn fields. Which great event called him again "into the field of wordy warfare", Edith?

EDITH. The execution of Charles I. He wrote "The Tenure of Kings and Magistrates", by which he desired to prove that the people might call to account a ruler who sets the law aside at his will.

MISS STEVENS. Salmasius, a professor of Leyden, and the most learned man in Europe, accused England of the murder of her king, and Milton now wrote a Latin reply.

MARY. "Defensio pro Populo Anglicano" in English "Defence for the People of England." I am always glad to air my Latin.

MISS STEVENS. Milton was told by the doctors that he would lose the sight of his right eye too — the sight of his left eye having gone long before this — if he wrote this work, but the love of his country was so great that he wrote the "Defensio" nevertheless, and he really became stone blind.

EDITH. But he retained his post as Latin secretary to the Council of State.

MISS STEVENS. Yes he did, and with a salary of £ 900 in our money. He was aided in his work. His wife died too, and the poor blind man, with his three little daughters, was very helpless indeed, so he married a second time, in 1656.

MARY. I read that his second wife died about fifteen months after their union, and that he had so deeply loved her for her goodness that he wrote a Sonnet on her, after having dreamt that she had come back to him.

MISS STEVENS. Milton wrote many Sonnets of which the one on "His Blindness" with the last line: "They also serve who only stand and wait", is very well known. Now the tide turned in Milton's life — What do I mean, Frances?

FRANCES. The Restoration brought gloom and terror to the Puritan poet's household. He was obliged to hide himself till the passing of the Act of Oblivion. Milton became poor. He had already begun "Paradise Lost", as "the inner eye, which no calamity could darken", as Macaulay says, "was opened".

FRANCES. Didn't Milton show it first to a Quaker friend who was most kind to him?

MISS STEVENS. Yes, to Thomas Ellwood. It was he who put the question, "But what of Paradise found?" after having perused the manuscript of Paradise Lost.

JANET. I see; this question led Milton to write "Paradise Regained". Did he not become wealthy again by the publications of these two grand poems?

MISS STEVENS. I am sorry to say no. He only received £ 10 for the finest poem in English Literature; his widow surrendered all her claims for the sum of £ 8.

MARY. What a shame! that makes £ 18.

MISS STEVENS. His last great poem, "Samson Agonistes", a choral drama, was written to meet the special doubts and trials of faith which, at this time, beset the great Puritan party. He strove to inspire his comrades with the same firm quiet trust in God which supported his own life. What did you read about the poet's later life, Edith?

EDITH. He lived at Bunhill Fields, London, in a small house. He used to get up at five in the morning; a chapter of the Hebrew Bible was read to him, after which he spent some time in quiet thought and communion with God. At seven he had breakfast — then till 12 o'clock he dictated either to his third wife, who nursed him very well, or to one of his daughters. These young women had become very learned, but very unruly too. He generally walked in the garden till one, when he dined. After dinner, he played on the organ, and at 2 he set to work again. At 6 o'clock he laid aside his work, and gave himself up to the enjoyment of pleasant talk with his family or with friends. At 8 he had a light supper, and soon after went to bed. Milton died November 8th 1674.

XVIII. "PARADISE LOST" AND "PARADISE REGAINED".

MISS STEVENS. You see there are three distinct periods in Milton's life; the first being the years spent in education, travel and study, the second, in which he strove to serve his country by his political writings, the third, the time of poverty and suffering, when he wrote his greatest poems.

Let us speak of the subject of "Paradise Lost". Who will tell it us briefly?

JANET. I will. It was given to me as a Sunday School Prize, and I read it. It begins with an invocation to the Holy Spirit. "What in me is dark, illumine; what is low, raise and support".

Then the action of the poem opens and we see the grand and terrible sight of the fallen angels lying thunderstruck in the lake of fire. Satan is the first to recover, and he tells them that open war is hopeless now, that they must work "by fraud and guile". In the second book, Satan passes out into "the realm of chaos" to seduce newly created men. Sin and Death have followed him, and "paved after him a broad and beaten way over the dark abyss", reaching from hell to earth. In the third book, we are taken to Heaven with its "pure sweet glory of light". We hear the voice of the Almighty speaking to His Son. God had made man free to keep His laws. He knows Satan's designs, and that man will fall by them. But Christ offers to raise man again to obedience, and to atone for sin by His own suffering and death. In the fourth book, Satan in the form of a cormorant approaches Paradise, which stands on a hill surrounded by a thick wood. He sees "flowers of all hues, without thorns the rose." Adam and Eve are taking their evening meal of fruit; Adam is speaking of the goodness of God. who has given them all, only keeping them "from the fruit of the forbidden tree". Satan sees at once how he can tempt them to disobey God. Uriel and Gabriel are sent to warn man; they make Satan "turn and fly with the shades of the night". In the fifth book, Eve has had a troubled dream, and Adam comforts her. After having offered up their morning prayers, they go forth to work in the garden. God sends Raphael to spend half of this day with Adam and Eve. In the sixth book Raphael begins to tell Adam of the rebellion of Satan and the war in Heaven. In the seventh, he gives an account of the creation down to the first Sabbath. In the eighth book, he explains to Adam the creation of the heavenly bodies. In the ninth, Eve goes out to work independently of Adam, who had told her that they are exposed to the Tempter. Satan takes the form of a Serpent, flatters her first, and then guides her "to the tree of knowledge of

4*

good and evil". She plucks the fruit and eats — then takes
a bough, laden with fruit, to Adam, and seduces him too.
In the tenth book, they receive their sentence. In the
eleventh, they repent and seek pardon. The Almighty accepts their repentance by foretelling the incarnation and death
of His Son.

In the 12th book, they are led forth (expelled) from
Paradise by the angel Michael.

"They hand in hand, with wandering steps and slow,
Through Eden took their solitary way".

MISS STEVENS. You have told it us very well indeed. Milton's purpose in the poem is to

"Assert eternal Providence,
And justify the ways of God to Man".

XIX. TIME OF THE RESTORATION.

MISS STEVENS. Four years after Milton's death appeared
another religious book, which is read in England almost as
much as the Bible. You all know which I mean.

FRANCES. The "Pilgrim's Progress" by John Bunyan, the
Puritan tinker. I loved to read it when I was a child even
before I understood the wonderful allegory.

MISS STEVENS. You are right, Frances; this book is the
joy of childhood and the solace of old age. One would not
imagine that Bunyan was in dark prison walls for having
preached the gospel in several Baptist congregations in Bed-
fordshire, when he wrote the adventures of Christian on his
journey towards the City of Pearls. I will give you a copy
with splendid illustrations of Christian at the Wicket Gate,
Christian at Vanity Fair, the Dark Valley — the Delectable
Mountain, the City of Destruction and so on, which I trust
will make an impression on you. We must conclude this
period by speaking of a burlesque poem which was the favourite book of Charles II.

MARY. "Hudibras" by Samuel Butler, "sprung from a
lowly stock."

MISS STEVENS. The adventures of Don Quixote. no doubt. suggested the idea of this work. Sir Hudibras, a Presbyterian knight, and his clerk, Squire Ralpho, sally forth to seek adventures and redress grievances, much as did the chivalrous knight of La Mancha and his trusty Sancho Panza. Charles II is said to have carried the book in his pocket wherever he went. Let us now speak of the great poet of this period. As it has often been said, the poetry of the Restoration was founded on intellect rather than on feeling. The poets were influenced by the stiff and dry Literature of France.

MARY. How very remarkable it is that the first poet of this new school was John Dryden. I can't bear him. Edith and I learned his "Ode for St. Cecilia's Day" or "Alexander's Feast".

MISS STEVENS. Perhaps you were too young to understand the beauty of it, for it is generally considered a fine piece of poetry, depicting the power of music. It is most happily illustrated in the succession of different passions and sentiments, in the mind of Alexander the Great, which the harper Timotheus excites by playing and singing

EDITH. The last line is: "He, (Timotheus) raised a mortal to the sky, she, (Cecilia) brought an angel down".

MISS STEVENS. I have a nice photograph of St. Cecilia and a copy of a big picture in the Dresden Gallery which I will show you to-night. Now I should like to hear the biography of the poet, whose best poem we have already criticised.

JANET. John Dryden was born in London in 1631; he was educated at Westminster School, and afterwards at Trinity College, Cambridge. His parents were Puritans, and so was he until the Restoration, when he became a Royalist. In 1663 he married the daughter of the Earl of Berkshire; were they happy together?

MISS STEVENS. The union is generally considered to have been an unhappy one. The poet was fickle, for on the accession of James II, he changed his religion, and became a Roman Catholic.

JANET. Did he think it an advantage?

MISS STEVENS. Indeed he found it very profitable. Soon after his conversion he was appointed Poet Laureate with a salary of £ 2000 a year.

MARY. Perhaps he thought like Henry IV of France: "Paris vaut bien une messe".

MISS STEVENS. Very likely; but one ought not to change one's religion for the sake of worldly gains. Those who do so cannot prosper, as we see in John Dryden too.

FRANCES. I know what you mean. At the Revolution Dryden was deprived of his office, but, nevertheless, he was considered as the "Prince of Critics" to the end of his life.

MISS STEVENS. When did he die, Mary?

MARY. He died with the century, that is in 1700, and was buried in Westminster Abbey in the Poets' Corner.

MISS STEVENS. Classify Dryden's writings, please, any one who can do so.

JANET. He wrote a satirical poem: "Absalom and Achitophel".

EDITH. What names! I shall never remember them.

MISS STEVENS. You have only to think of the biblical story — I trust you know it.

EDITH. Now I see; at first I thought they were Greek heroes.

MISS STEVENS. Under these Bible names, Dryden attacked several well known persons of the court for the attempt they were making to exclude the King's brother from the succession; but he wrote a second satirical poem, you said, Janet.

JANET. "Mac Flecknoe", a literary satire.

MISS STEVENS. Besides these he wrote two controversial poems, one called "Religio Laici", in which he defends the English Church from the attacks of her enemies, and the "Hind and Panther", which was written in defence of the efforts made by James II to restore the Roman Catholic Church.

MARY. I should like to know "which is which"; first he defends one church then another; how very queer!

MISS STEVENS. The Church of England is represented by the Panther", "the fairest creature of the spotted kind"; he exhibits his new-born affection for the church of his adoption which he paints as "a milk white hind immortal and unchanged".

FRANCES. Didn't Dryden undertake a translation of Virgil as well?

MISS STEVENS. He did, but although he received £ 1200 for it, as he had spent three toilsome years in turning "the Georgics" and "the Æneid" into English pentameters, his version is very inferior to the original.

Dryden is remarkable as a dramatist; he attempted to introduce French Tragedies, but the experiment proved a failure.

MISS STEVENS. Before we talk of the next Period of English Literature, I will tell you how the Royal Society was founded. By the way, do you know which society I mean, Janet?

JANET. I suppose the Royal Society of Astronomy, Chemistry, Physiology, Medicine, etc. which still meets in London.

MISS STEVENS. The very same. Strange to say, whilst the Civil War, with its religious and political struggles absorbed the country, a few men, apart from the strife, and who cared for scientific matters, met at one another's houses. Out of this knot arose "the Royal Society": Astronomy, Chemistry etc. were all founded as studies, and the literature of these sciences was begun in the age of the Restoration. You all know which great scientist lived at the time of the Revolution.

MARY. I know — Sir Isaac Newton. I read some anecdotes about him.

MISS STEVENS. Tell us the anecdotes another time. I mention this great man among the literary men of England, because he laid two great works before the Royal Society; one on the "Theory of Light" — the other, in which he established certain laws you have heard of in your science class, he called "Principles".

FRANCES. In this work he established the law of gravitation — our science-master told us, that he found it out by watching the movements of a pendulum.

MISS STEVENS. There is another great philosopher, who has been thought and spoken of very much of late. I don't think you ever heard his name. It is John Locke.

MARY. What a funny name — I shall think of a lock to remember him.

MISS STEVENS. His name is written with an e at the end; no more nonsense now, Mary please!

John Locke wrote an "Essay concerning the Human Understanding", in which his leading doctrine is the double origin of our knowledge, namely sensation and reflection. I daresay you wouldn't understand anything about it, if I read you some chapter, but all people taking an interest in education study this clever work.

XX. THE AUGUSTAN AGE.

MISS STEVENS. Why has the age of Queen Anne been called the "Augustan Age", Frances?

FRANCES. Because the writings of the great authors were so distinguished for refinement that the age resembled that of Augustus.

MISS STEVENS. Who stands at the head of these "Wits"?

JANET. Alexander Pope was born in London in 1688; he was the son of a wealthy linendraper. After Alexander's birth, his father retired from business and lived at Binfield in the neighbourhood of Windsor Forest.

MISS STEVENS. It was a wise thing that the father chose this beautiful scenery for his deformed and precocious little son, who was already a poet in the nursery, but a very fretful and delicate child. Janet, please, go on.

JANET. Pope's father was a Roman Catholic, so his education was for the most part conducted by priests. When he was only about 19, his public career as a poet began. I don't know which was his first production.

MISS STEVENS. The "Ode to Solitude" which he even wrote before 19; then he produced "the Essay on Criticism" which was more like the work of an old and experienced poet than that of so young a man as Pope then was.

JANET. I learned some lines from it:

"A little learning is a dangerous thing
Drink deep or taste not the Pierian spring,
There shallow draughts intoxicate the brain,
And drinking largely sobers us again."

MISS STEVENS. The "Rape of the Lock" is usually considered the best of Pope's poems. It has been called "a dwarf
epic", having for its subject the cutting of a lock of hair
from the head of a beautiful Court-maiden; in the poem she
is called "Belinda". In the first canto, she is warned by
the spirit Ariel that something dreadful is going to happen.
In the second canto the old baron who has determined to
have the lock of hair is described. In the third canto, we
have a coffee-drinking at Hampton Court, where the baron
succeeds in obtaining a pair of scissors.

In the fourth canto, Belinda is in an agony of sorrow,
and begs for the return of the lock of hair from the baron,
but in vain. In canto V a fearful fight takes place among
the ladies and gentlemen of the Court. Belinda is determined
to get back the stolen lock; she flies at the Baron, and flings
snuff at him, and makes him sneeze frightfully. Suddenly
the lock vanishes, and takes its place among the constellations.
— Addison called this poem a "delicious little thing". You
see he was right.

FRANCES. Was the court-maiden really bereft of her lock?

MISS STEVENS. The ringlet of a court-maiden, Miss Ara-
bella Fermor, had indeed been stolen by her lover, Lord Petre,
and the silly trick led to a coolness between the family of
the delinquent and the injured fair one. Pope set to work, inspired by the wish to reconcile the estranged lovers by a
hearty laugh.

MARY. I am sure he succeeded.

MISS STEVENS. This poem is interesting too because we
get a clear and vivid impression of what was then fashionable
life. Pope had a great admiration for Dryden, who had, as
you remember, "the drawing-room method of expression", besides "the long resounding line". But I should like to hear
more of Pope's life and other works.

EDITH. He translated the "Iliad" of Homer; is it a good
translation?

MISS STEVENS. No, on the contrary, a very bad one. The great scholar Bentley, upon the volume sent to him by the poet wrote: "It is a pretty poem, but you must not call it Homer".

The heroes are gentlemen of the fashionable life of Queen Anne's reign. Nevertheless the poet pocketed more than £ 8000 for his translation.

EDITH. I see now how he could afford to buy the pretty country-seat at Twickenham on the banks of the Thames with the famous grotto.

MISS STEVENS. It must be said that he was very hospitable; first of all he took in his aged mother after his father's death. Then he welcomed all his literary friends there.

MARY. Who were these friends, pray? I should like to know their names.

MISS STEVENS. You will get to know some of them better; they were first Joseph Addison and Jonathan Swift, of whom we shall speak. Then Henry St. John, Viscount Bolingbroke.

JANET. Who was the friend of Voltaire — how interesting!

EDITH. Was Pope ever married?

MISS STEVENS. No, Pope never married, but he delighted in female society. He was in love for some time with Lady Mary Wortley Montague, but suddenly his feelings changed.

JANET. Is she the lady of letter-writing renown?

MISS STEVENS. Yes, the very same.

She called her quondam swain, the "wicked wasp of Twickenham". Which are Pope's last works?

FRANCES. He wrote "the Dunciad", a fierce poetical satire against the would-be poets of his time, who pestered him.

MARY. What a rude name! I should think they resented being called dunces.

MISS STEVENS. Pope did not mind that; he criticised the trifling education of the day as well. He also wrote the "Essay on Man", the teaching of which we must in part condemn, but we cannot but admire the versification.

JANET. I remember one line: "The proper study of mankind is man".

EDITH. Didn't he also publish an edition of Shakespeare?

MISS STEVENS. Yes, he did, but he left out everything he thought indecent or coarse. Pope grew very peevish and ill-tempered on account of his ill-health. He himself calls his life "one long disease". When did he die, Frances?

FRANCES. In 1744, at the age of fifty-six.

MISS STEVENS. Some one said of him: "He was dwarfish in stature but great in genius".

XXI. JONATHAN SWIFT.

MISS STEVENS. One of Pope's intimate friends was Swift, of whose unhappy life you read in the little preface to "Gulliver's Travels" in the schoolroom. You might tell me the chief facts of it.

EDITH. Jonathan Swift was born in 1667 in Dublin, but his parents were English. His father died even before he was born, so he was dependent on the charity of his relations. His uncle sent him to Kilkenny School and then to Trinity College, Dublin. After his uncle's death, he found shelter at Moor Park in the house of Sir William Temple, with whom his mother was slightly connected. Was he happy there?

MISS STEVENS. He could not feel happy. Sir William treated him little better than a servant, and often even sneered at his poor relative and secretary. Swift being of a proud disposition could neither forgive nor forget this treatment. "It was bitter bread he ate", some one said, "looking out into the dim future for the time when he could break his chains and smite tenfold for every stripe he had received".

EDITH. But Sir William Temple gave him the means of graduating as M. A. at Oxford, and then made him his secretary.

MISS STEVENS. In Sir William's house, Swift got to know Hester, the daughter of the housekeeper. She is better known in Literature by the name of Stella. It is said that Swift was married to her privately, but there can be no certainty as to that.

MARY. How horrid of him to break her heart: now I don't like him any more.

MISS STEVENS. Dear child, he was severely punished for it, at we shall see. Go on, Edith.

EDITH. He entered the Church, and obtained a small living in Ireland.

MISS STEVENS. But he often came over to England where his society was much coveted — on account of his cleverness and wit.

JANET. You told us last time that he often visited Pope. Was he a Whig or a Tory?

MISS STEVENS. At first he joined the Whig Party, and wrote smart papers in their defence, until, finding they did not reward him sufficiently, he became a Tory.

FRANCES. How very fickle; fancy, changing one's colours; but was he not disappointed again?

MISS STEVENS. He was, as he only received the deanery of St. Patrick's in Dublin instead of a bishopric.

MARY. Served him right. I suppose he became a Whig again when he thought it more to his advantage?

MISS STEVENS. On the accession of George I, the Whigs came into favour again; he left London where he had been helping the Tory ministry and went back to Dublin.

Do you know what he did then to make himself popular?

JANET. He wrote the "Letters of M. B. Drapier" against the English government for their bad treatment of Ireland; by them the Dean became the idol of the Irish nation.

MISS STEVENS. All attempts to bring Swift to trial were unsuccessful, though everybody knew that the Dean and Drapier were the same man. He had an unbounded influence over the rabble.

FRANCES. He had taken their part against the English, and so they were glad to take his.

MISS STEVENS. After the death of Stella, he went into melancholy — and ended by becoming insane.

EDITH. How very sad!

MISS STEVENS. He didn't get one minute's rest — for ten hours a day, the grey-haired lunatic hurried up and down the chamber as if it were a cage, and he a chained wild beast. I told you Stella was well avenged. He died in 1745. We will mention the "Tale of a Tub" first, as it had already appeared in 1704. Do you know the contents of "Gulliver's Travels", Janet?

JANET. Gulliver is a ship's surgeon, who undertakes four voyages; firstly he pays a visit to Lilliput, where the inhabitants are only six inches high; secondly he goes to Brobdignag, where there are only giants. Then he gets to Laputa, a flying island, and from there to another island, where there is a city with an absurd academy, where knowledge is imparted to the students by making them swallow it in wafers, like pills, then to an unpronounceable island, Glubbdubdrib, where magicians live, and finally to a fourth island, Luggnagg, where the wretched people continue living after having lost the power of enjoying life.

MARY. May I tell about the fourth journey? It is to the country of the Honyhuhums, where the horses are so intelligent, it is so amusing! They rule better than human beings, the Jahoos.

MISS STEVENS. Child, please do stop! You do not know that Swift hated his fellow-creatures so bitterly that he describes some of them as being degraded to the rank of untamable brutes.

MARY. Oh, I begin to see! I only looked upon the Voyages of W. Gulliver as a series of wonderful adventures. I have often wished he had invited me to go with him — now it is all only a satire!

MISS STEVENS. Not only that — there are some useful lessons to be learned for willing learners in the first three voyages.

MARY. Lessons for grown up people? Must they still learn lessons?

MISS STEVENS. We never stop learning lessons, Mary — life is one long school. These lessons Swift teaches us are on patriotism, science and learning. I will add that his style is remarkable for its Anglo-Saxon expressiveness. Now we will speak of another better-tempered prose-writer of Queen Anne's reign, whom you know well.

MISS STEVENS. It is the author of "Robinson Crusoe". — His name is known all over the world, Mary!

MARY. Daniel Defoe.

MISS STEVENS. Tell us what you know of his life.

FRANCES. He was the son of a London butcher and was born in 1631; first he was educated to become a Dissenting minister, but he took to trade instead, and was a hosier and tilemaker and woollen draper by turns. He began to write political pamphlets to defend the Whigs and Dissenters, but he got into trouble and was fined over and over again, and at last imprisoned; for attacking the government he suffered in the pillory. Then he bethought himself, gave up writing satirical pamphlets, and wrote his beautiful novels.

MISS STEVENS. "Robinson Crusoe", although a work of fiction, is founded on the story of Alexander Selkirk. the sailor who spent years of solitude on the Isle of Juan Fernandez. As you all know Robinson and Friday's history, we will pass on. Defoe wrote a great many books, about 210. You read some chapters of the "Journal of the great Plague in London". which describes scenes that never took place, but are nevertheless true to the life. Do you know if he became rich by his writings?

JANET. No, he did not; he was in hiding for the last two years of his life, for he was always afraid of being sent to jail by his creditors.

MISS STEVENS. Indeed he did not even die (1731) in his own house, which he had built at Stoke Newington. He was buried at Bunhill Fields, where Milton had lived. It may be said of him, that his interests were wide and patriotic rather than personal, and that his own affairs had been neglected in his work for others' good.

—

XXII. THE FIRST ESSAYISTS.

MISS STEVENS. There are two great friends who have the merit of having perfected the English prose-style.

FRANCES. Richard Steele and Joseph Addison; they were great "chums" at the Charterhouse School where my brother Percy is now, but Steele must have been an unsteady fellow in later life.

MISS STEVENS. He was born at Dublin in 1671, ten years later than Defoe. From the Charterhouse where he fell in with Addison, as you said, he went to Oxford; his uncle promised him an estate, if he would persevere in his studies, but this did not suit him, so he joined the army. He did not set a good example to his inferiors; he lived a gay and careless life. His wife brought him a fortune, but money was like water in his hands, he could not keep it.

FRANCES. That's why he fled to Wales to be safe from his persecutors. poor man — he even died there in 1729; but how did he come to write political Essays?

MISS STEVENS. He held the post of Government Gazetteer for some time, and the idea occurred to him that a paper might be published for the people who were so anxious to hear all about the war going on in Spain, and about many other things which might interest the common people. While at College, he had already begun to write some works in connection with his friend Addison, whose life is, as some one said, "a stainless one".

MISS STEVENS. What do you know of Addison, Frances?

FRANCES. Joseph Addison was born in 1767 in Wiltshire, and educated at the Charterhouse where he made friends with Steele. At Oxford he was already distinguished for his poetical abilities, as every guide-book tells us.

MISS STEVENS. Through Lord Somers he received a pension which enabled him to travel on the Continent.

JANET. But didn't he lose this pension when William and Mary ascended the throne?

MISS STEVENS. Yes, he did, but in Queen Anne's reign the Government employed him to write a poem in praise of Marlborough's victories. The comparison of Marlborough to an angel directing the storm, made the great general very popular. The author was well rewarded for the fine poem by the Government. He was raised to an important position, he became Chief Secretary of Ireland.

JANET. Was it here that he began to write his political essays with his friend Steele?

MISS STEVENS. Steele had already begun to write the "Tatler" three times a week. Addison contributed some papers to it, not many though. He started the "Spectator" after the "Tatler" was discontinued. It was issued daily.

EDITH. Was it a daily newspaper in the modern sense?

MISS STEVENS. No; its great feature was not the latest political news in the "leading articles" as in our papers; but it was an elegantly written Essay on some social, literary, or philosophical subject, and its charm lay in its sparkling wit and quaint humour, or delicate criticism.

MARY. Were not the contributors supposed to be members of the "Spectator Club"?

MISS STEVENS. Yes, they were types or representatives of varied characters. There were, besides Mr. Spectator himself, Sir Roger de Coverley, the simple-minded country-gentleman, Sir Andrew Freeport, the London Merchant or Cityman, Captain Sentry, the Armyman, the learned Templar, and the thoughtful Clergyman.

MARY. The gem of the noble group is Sir Roger de Coverley; this good old bachelor is one of the nicest heroes we find in books. We adore the dance called after him.

MISS STEVENS. Addison is certainly the painter of the full length portrait of Sir Roger de Coverley as well as the writer of the "Essay on Milton" and the "Vision of Mirza", which are the finest specimens of what Addison's graceful pen could do. He began a third periodical "The Guardian" which was at once read all over England; its circulation was immense. I will read to you some passages from it in the drawing-room. Addison could now afford to buy an estate near Rugby. In 1713 he put his tragedy of "Cato" on the Stage, and Pope wrote the Prologue to it.

FRANCES. Did this tragedy have a great success?

MISS STEVENS. A very great one; it was played for 35 nights in succession. To-day it is not so much thought of, as it is written quite in the French style.

JANET. What a pity he copied the stiff French writers; why didn't he copy Shakespeare?

MISS STEVENS. I am sorry to say Shakespeare was not half appreciated at that time. — Pope, who was for some time on very intimate terms with Addison, praised "Cato" very highly. But continue Addison's life, Mary.

MARY. He married a grand lady, the Countess of Warwick, in 1716. but the high-born lady's temper prevented her husband from having anything like domestic happiness.

MISS STEVENS. I believe that the marriage was a happy one, in spite of rumours to the contrary. Addison wrote that beautiful hymn you like to sing so much:

"When all thy mercies, oh my God,
My rising soul surveys,
Transported with the view,
I'm lost in wonder, love and praise."

JANET. I didn't know it was by Addison. I read that Addison had a step-son, the Earl of Warwick, and that this wild fellow gave him no end of trouble. Is that true?

MISS STEVENS. Perfectly true, and when Addison was on his death-bed, he sent for this thoughtless youth, so that he might see "how peacefully a Christian could die". When did his death take place?

FRANCES. On June 17th 1719; he was buried by night in Westminster Abbey.

MISS STEVENS. You will see his statue there over his tomb when we go up to London.

XXIII. THE FIRST ENGLISH NOVEL WRITERS.

MISS STEVENS. Now that a good prose style had been developed, a new prose literature began, Novel-writing. Does one of you know which is the first English novel?

JANET. I think "Pamela" or "Virtue Rewarded" by Samuel Richardson. (1689—1761.)

MISS STEVENS. It appeared in 1740, and was received with a real storm of delight by the public. "Clarissa Harlowe" and "Sir Charles Grandison" followed; they are each written in a series of letters, and are intended to give pictures of life in the lower, middle, and upper classes of society.

MARY. May we read one of them?

MISS STEVENS. When you are older, you may. It requires a good deal of patience to read them; they are tedious by their extreme length and the minuteness of their descriptions. A parody of "Pamela" soon followed, written by the second novelist of this period.

FRANCES. "Joseph Andrews" by Henry Fielding, 1707—1754. My former English master used to say: you need only remember this novel and, "Tom Jones" by Fielding, another humorous novel.

MISS STEVENS. Fielding led a gay and dissipated life. Money was spent as fast as it was earned, whilst Richardson spent his life first in hard work, and then in pleasant retirement. "Tom Jones" was imitated by the third novel-writer of this period, a countryman of yours, Janet.

JANET. "Tobias Smollett". (1721—1771); he wrote "Roderick Random."

MISS STEVENS. Just like "Tom Jones", a humorous and interesting novel, but often exaggerated and unnatural. I must mention a clergyman of the Church of England, Lawrence Sterne, as another novel-writer of this period. He wrote Tristram Shandy; and after a tour on the Continent, the "Sentimental Journey", which is full of frivolity and eccentricities. The best moral novel of this period was written by Dr. Samuel Johnson.

FRANCES. You mean "Rasselas" — a tale of Abyssinia.

MISS STEVENS. Such is the title, but the author makes no attempt to identify himself with oriental modes of thought. We will hear his biography.

EDITH. Dr. Samuel Johnson was born in 1709 at Lichfield; he was the son of a bookseller. — He went to Oxford, but his father died, and he was obliged to leave the university. He took to teaching, but had very few pupils.

MISS STEVENS. Still he had one very clever pupil, no less than David Garrick. Garrick had first studied to become a barrister. It is said that both master and pupil went up to London to seek their fortune.

MARY. Who was the more lucky, master or pupil?

MISS STEVENS. The pupil; he became the most famous actor of the day, whilst Johnson's path was a hard and perilous one. He had to endure the worst miseries of the miserable literary life of those days.

EDITH. Poor man! Didn't he get much money from his publisher for the periodical Essays, "the Rambler" and the "Idler".

MISS STEVENS. Not enough to enable him to live comfortably. It must be owned that Dr. Johnson was too benevolent also; even when he himself was poor, his house was an asylum for destitute people.

MARY. Just like Oliver Goldsmith: they were great friends, were they not? "Birds of a feather flock together."

MISS STEVENS. The kind-hearted Dr. Johnson was better off after he had completed his greatest work; which is it?

JANET. The "Dictionary of the English Language".

MISS STEVENS. It is a great work for his time, but it was necessarily imperfect, especially in etymology. Johnson published an Edition of Shakespeare with a very fine preface. He wrote another well-known work.

EDITH. "Lives of the Poets" — is it a good book?

MISS STEVENS. The book is a very unsafe guide. Johnson's view of writing poetry consisted in the making of high-sounding verse, and smooth rhymes; our taste differs from his. Let us finish his life.

JANET. In 1762 Johnson received a pension of £ 300 a year from George III. When he was better off, he began to travel about, he visited the Western Isles of Scotland, and went to see the sights of Paris. He died in London in 1784, and joined the illustrious company of those who sleep under the stones of Westminster Abbey.

XXIV. OLIVER GOLDSMITH.

MISS STEVENS. Dr. Johnson's great friend was Oliver Goldsmith. I know you are quite familiar with his life and with his chief works.

MARY. Please may I tell you his life? I think it is so interesting.

MISS STEVENS. If you like, but only mention the chief items.

5*

MARY. Oliver Goldsmith was born in 1728 at Pallas in the country of Longford in Ireland. He was sent by his uncle to Trinity College, Dublin, where he cared little for studies, but more for ballad writing. He was fond of stealing out at night to hear his ballads sung in the streets, so he often got into scrapes.

MISS STEVENS. But the good-natured student gave most of the hard-earned money to the beggars who beset him on the way. Go on please.

MARY. In 1752, Goldsmith went to Edinburgh to study medicine; then he went to Leyden and from there he started for a grand tour through Flanders, France, Germany, Switzerland, and Italy, "with a guinea in his pocket, but one shirt to his back, and a flute in his hand". By performing on his flute in the streets of the towns and villages he passed through, he was able to pay his way from place to place.

MISS STEVENS. But when he got back to England, he was as poor as ever, poor fellow! What did he do to gain his livelihood? We had better let your sister go on.

EDITH. First he was a chemist's assistant, then a doctor to the poor, then a teacher.

MISS STEVENS. It is supposed that Goldsmith had been an usher in a school before he went abroad.

EDITH. Finally he became a bookseller's hack, until at last, his works became popular. Now money poured in upon him. Notwithstanding which he was never out of debt.

MISS STEVENS. He loved fine dress and extravagant ways of living too — besides, he was so foolishly generous that he could keep nothing from the beggars who were ever prowling about him.

EDITH. When he died in 1774, he left a debt of £ 2000 behind him.

MISS STEVENS. I know you have all read the "Vicar of Wakefield" although it is rather a long story to read, and not such a favourite book with us as it used to be. We like short novels best. But the story of this country gentleman and his family of six children is told with such simple feeling and charming humour, that we cannot but feel interested in their doings. Which passages did you like best, Janet?

JANET. I think the family picture most amusing, but I like Moses going to the fair and selling the old horse.

MISS STEVENS. I will not forget to say that Goldsmith wished to set before the world a more just estimate of things, than that which prevails in the world, and to win admiration for what was really noble and heroic. In a little preface, Goldsmith says "The hero of this piece unites in himself the three greatest characters upon earth. He is a priest, a husbandman, and the father of a family. He is drawn as ready to teach and ready to obey, as simple in affluence and majestic in adversity." You learned part of the "Traveller", which Goldsmith wrote after his continental tour, and part of the "Deserted Village". Which do you prefer?

ALL. Oh, "Sweet Auburn, loveliest village of the plain."

MISS STEVENS. He wrote a comedy which had great success too.

EDITH. "She Stoops to Conquer"; it was first acted in 1773. I read he had written another comedy first: the "Goodnatured Man" which was not so well received.

MISS STEVENS. "She Stoops to Conquer" holds its place on the stage at the present day, as one of the best specimens of old English comedy.

XXV. PROSE WRITERS OF THE REIGN OF GEORGE III.

MISS STEVENS. History shared in the progress made in prose-writing, and was raised to the rank of literature by three contemporaries; only all of them were influenced by the French School of Montesquieu and Voltaire; two of them were Scotchmen. Of course, you know them, Janet.

JANET. First David Hume (1711—1776) who wrote the "History of England". Is it still much read now-a-days?

MISS STEVENS. For ease, beauty, and picturesque power of style, there is nothing like it in the range of English historical literature, and for these qualities it yet holds an honoured place on our book-shelves. Yet the day of Hume as an authority on English History has long gone by, I will read you the Chapter on the "Death of Queen Elizabeth". — Who is the second Scotch historian, Edith?

EDITH. William Robertson (1721—1793); he first wrote the "History of Scotland" which treats of the reigns of Mary Stuart and James VI of Scotland and I of England.

MISS STEVENS. It is very likely that the great German poet, Schiller, took from Robertson's "History of Scotland" the subject of his tragedy "Maria Stuart".

FRANCES. Which side does Robertson take?

MISS STEVENS. He does not take any side; he relates in pure, pathetic and dignified language the history of the unhappy Queen; he neither makes a martyr of her, nor does he brand her as a beautiful criminal. It is the right position; a historian ought to be impartial. But Robertson wrote two other Histories; which are they?

FRANCES. "The History of the Emperor Charles V" and the "History of the Discovery of America".

MISS STEVENS. The story of Columbus fascinated him, and nowhere, perhaps, have we a finer specimen of stately narrative. We might read some chapters of this history, and you will admire its clear style. — Now we come to the greatest of "the Historic triad", Edward Gibbon. It was at Rome that he conceived the idea of his great work. You will know the title?

FRANCES. "The Decline and Fall of the Roman Empire." Didn't Gibbon (1737—1794) become a Roman Catholic at Oxford?

MISS STEVENS. Yes he did. At Lausanne, where he resided for a long time, he returned to the Protestant religion, but finally he became a sceptic.

EDITH. How many centuries does this History embrace?

MISS STEVENS. Nearly thirteen; it is a gigantic work; it gives us not only the history of the two great branches of the Roman Empire, but of all the various nations that played a part in the grand drama of which Rome and Constantinople were the centres. — Here we must mention Edward Burke (1730—1797). Who was he, Mary?

MARY. The splendid Irish orator, the ornament of the House of Commons for 28 years, who wrote "Reflections on the French Revolution".

MISS STEVENS. In that work, he warned Englishmen against cherishing at home the ideas which were bearing such terrible fruit on the other side of the Channel. We shall read some chapters of the "Reflections" together. The work was sold by tens of thousands. No political essay ever produced so extraordinary an effect.

JANET. Wasn't Sheridan (1751—1816), the Dramatist, Burke's friend?

MISS STEVENS. He supported him in the Trial of Warren Hastings. Sheridans powers as an orator were scarcely inferior to those of Burke. Unfortunately he was extravagant in his way of living and not unfrequently his rooms were occupied by his creditors, waiting for cash, which they were not to receive. Which are his two greatest plays?

MARY. The "School for Scandal" and the "Rivals".

MISS STEVENS. The former is a very witty production, showing the mischievous result of gossip; the latter is one of the most humorous comedies.

JANET. I read the "Rivals", and felt very highly amused with Mrs. Malaprop who constantly mixes up words similar in sound.

XXVI. THE POETS OF NATURE.

MISS STEVENS. There is a French saying "on revient toujours à ses premières amours"; we might apply it to the period in Literature we are beginning to-day. The Poets of the 18th century return to Nature. They describe very truthfully their impressions derived from Nature itself. Who is the first of these poets, Edith?

EDITH. James Thomson, a Scotchman; he wrote "The Seasons" and "Rule Britannia".

MISS STEVENS. "The Seasons" brought into the artificial life of the town the scent of field flowers, the murmur of brooks and summer breezes, and gleams of the glory of sunrise and sunset. The poet gives man his true place in the midst of Nature.

FRANCES. Haven't they been set to music?

MISS STEVENS. They have — by Haydn, the German musician; when they are performed again here, I will take you to hear them.

The love of simplicity finds expression in the poetry of William Cowper. What do you know of him, Janet?

JANET. Poor man! He was born in 1713. His father was a clergyman, his mother died when the very sensitive boy was only six years old. He was sent to a boarding-school where he suffered greatly on account of his timidity. When he was preparing for an examination to get the position of Clerk of the Journals of the House of Lords, his nervous terror became so great that he became insensible. When his mind began to recover, a kind friend, Mrs. Unwin took him into her house; for more than twenty years she watched over Cowper with unceasing care, and did all she could to cheer him. After Mrs. Unwin's death, Cowper sank into a state of melancholy again from which he never recovered. He lingered on through three sad years, till he was released from all suffering in May 1800.

MARY. I shouldn't have thought that the author of "John Gilpin", "the citizen of famous London town" who had the desperate ride, was a melancholy man.

MISS STEVENS. It was a friend of Mrs. Unwin's, Lady Austen, who told Cowper the story of John Gilpin one evening, when she found him in a melancholy mood; she persuaded him too that he ought to write another poem in blank verse, and gave him the sofa for a subject. He obeyed, and after having recently sung of "Truth", "Hope" and "Charity" he sang of "the Sofa". He wrote other poems besides, which, Frances?

FRANCES. The "Olney Hymns" and other descriptive and didactic poems. The first part of the "Sofa" is the "Task" in which he censures luxury and dissipation.

MISS STEVENS. He wrote too "Table Talks", and he made excellent Translations. Besides, he was one of the most charming letter-writers; his style is as easy and artless in his correspondence as in his poetry.

Another poet describes his life in the country, his home, his friends, the life of the poor.

JANET. You mean George Crabbe (1754—1832), a country clergyman, who wrote the "Village and the Parish Register", rather sad stories about the poor.

MISS STEVENS. Yes, sad, but only too true, as we say. You remember no doubt "the Parish Workhouse", which I read to you once. Who else helped forward the taste for natural poetry?

JANET. Thomas Percy, Bishop of Dromore. He published "Percy's Reliques" some of which commemorate the bravery of heroes such as Douglas.

MARY. Are they a literary forgery too, like Macpherson's "Ossian"?

MISS STEVENS. No, they are a collection of ballads, which have been handed down by tradition.

XXVII. ROBERT BURNS.

MISS STEVENS. Another element, the passionate treatment of love, had on the whole been absent from our poetry since the Restoration. It was restored by the greatest of lyric poets, a Scotch ploughman. Who was he?

JANET. Robert Burns, of whom we are just as proud as of Sir Walter Scott. Some one has even called him "The Shakespeare of Scotland". He was born on January 25 th 1759 at Alloway in Ayrshire, where his father had a small farm. Burns left school at the age of eleven, as he had to help his father in farming. But the poet increased his knowledge by studying all the books within his reach.

MISS STEVENS. They were not so many: Addison, Pope, Allan Ramsay, a Scotch pastoral poet, Thomson, Sterne, and Mackenzie, a Scotch novelist. As he went whistling behind his plough, thoughts of nature and its beauties, of love and its tender emotions, would gradually shape themselves into words and rhythms, such as would exactly suit the very tunes he was whistling. Thus song-making was his earliest effort as a poet.

MARY. It was then he was inspired to write the "Field Mouse" and "To a Mountain Daisy", two sweet poems.

MISS STEVENS. Poems like those are true wildflowers, breathing a delicate fragrance, such as the blossoms of no cultured garden can ever boast. When did the poet publish his first volume, Edith?

EDITH. In 1786, when farming had become so bad that he wanted to sail for Jamaica; he desired to raise the needful funds and to leave some lasting memorial of himself — and so he had 600 copies of his poems printed. The little volume sold rapidly, and the poet abandoned his idea of emigrating. He accepted the invitation of the great people of Edinburgh to pay them a visit.

MISS STEVENS. They made an extraordinary fuss about him; he became the lion of the day and, strange to say, the ploughman conducted himself as well as the finest gentleman among them — but when the gloss had worn off their plaything, and some fresh novelty had sprung up among them, this man, whose poetry has spread its sweetness into every Scotch home, was looked on coldly, neglected and forgotten. The rest of his life-story is a tale of deep sadness and had better be told briefly, Frances.

FRANCES. With the £ 500 which he cleared by the second edition of his poems, Burns took the farm of Ellisland, near Dumfries. He married in 1788. Some time afterwards, he obtained the office of exciseman for the district in which he lived.

In 1791 he gave up the farm, and went to live at Dumfries. His employment was very bad for him; he took to drink, and died at the age of 37, in 1796, leaving his wife with six children, in poverty. 1200 persons attended his funeral.

MISS STEVENS. The faults of the man are forgotten or at least forgiven. His memory is dear to his countrymen for the sake of his poetry. You mentioned two of his poems; which are the others?

JANET. "To Mary in Heaven" or "Highland Mary", in memory of Mary Campbell, to whom he was engaged to be married, but who died.

MARY. "John Anderson, my Joy", "My Heart's in the Highlands". If he had only written that latter poem, he would have been immortal, for it is a lovely song.

MISS STEVENS. You must read the "Cotter's Saturday Night", a beautiful domestic idyll, a faithful picture of Scottish peasant life.

And later on the "Jolly Beggars", a poem of mad revelry, and "Tam o' Shanter", a weird serio-comic tale which displays the versatility of his genius, and raises him to the highest rank among British bards.

Let me add that, in the last year of the 18th century, a young poet, Thomas Campbell, wrote "The Pleasures of Hope", a bright outlook into the coming era.

What did he write later on?

EDITH. "Hohenlinden" The "Battle of the Baltic", and the splendid war poem "Ye Mariners of England that guard our native seas."

XXVIII. THE "LAKE POETS".

MISS STEVENS. As we begin the 19th century, we find that the strong force, which was leading men to question and cast off authority, had not lost its energy. It is like the springing up of a new life which cannot be stifled or crushed. The wild destroying power could only be controlled, as men found out, by the rule of reason and conscience. It was the noblest and most enlightened which saw this first. And of these William Wordsworth (1770—1850) stands as the leader in the great battle of the 19th century. He was supported by two friends in his wish to return to nature. Do you know them?

JANET. Samuel Taylor Coleridge (1772—1834) and Robert Southey (1774—1843). The three brother poets resided near Lake Windermere in Cumberland; for this reason they have been named the "Lake Poets".

MISS STEVENS. All three of them sympathised keenly in their youth with the principles of the French Revolution. Wordsworth even lived in France for some time, hoping to help the Revolution onwards to its true result. His heart had been deeply wounded by the bitter failure of his dreams, but he did not look at human nature with a hopeless sneer.

On the contrary, in all his poems he illustrates the oneness of Nature with man, and of both with God.

EDITH. I read somewhere that his "Lyrical Ballads" were the subjects of constant ridicule — that even parodies were written on them.

MARY. I don't wonder. "We are Seven" is a stupid little piece of poetry!

MISS STEVENS. It was perhaps natural that at first people, missing the ordinary trappings of poetry, cried out that the strivings were childish and the language prose, but as they came to look more into the very heart of things, they began to see the deep immortal poetry of the "Lyrical Ballads" in the thought which is the soul of each. So you are quite mistaken Mary. Which are Wordsworth's greatest poems?

FRANCES. "The Excursion", "The Prelude", and "The White Doe of Rylstone".

MISS STEVENS. The "Excursion" is a philosophical poem; the poet takes a walk and meets first with a Scotch pedlar, who converses only too well for a man in his position, about truth, beauty, love and hope; then he meets a solitary man whose temper has been soured by continual disappointment — then he visits a clergyman who relates interesting stories about the people who had lived and died in his parish. Afterwards he visits a neighbouring lake. Which poem of Coleridge's do you know?

EDITH. The "Ancient Mariner", a story which the old mariner himself tells a wedding guest. A vessel leaves a sea-port town; the voyage is prosperous till the mariner shoots an albatross, a bird which seamen consider a sign of good fortune. Now the ship remains motionless in a quiet sea, where the sun glows like a ball of fire — the crew all die of thirst, the mariner alone is spared. He repents of the evil he has done, and angelic spirits, pitying him, make the dead bodies rise to their feet. They hoist the sails, the ship moves on, and, at length, she nears the mariner's native land.

He is rescued by the pilot, who puts off from shore to him. The agonies he often endures are unbearable, and his heart burns within him till his ghastly tale is told.

MISS STEVENS. Coleridge was a student of German Literature, and loved wild stories of the old Teutonic legends. He was a little wild in his youth, but toned down later on. In 1804 he delivered his celebrated "Lectures on Shakespeare". He translated Schiller's "Wallenstein" into English, and wrote other poems of which the "Hymn Before Sunrise in the Vale of Chamounix" is well known. What do you know of Southey and his works, Janet?

JANET. He wrote so much that he overworked himself and became childish.

MARY. What a warning! "Mary, the maid of the Inn" is not a long poem however.

JANET. His greatest poem is the "Curse of Kehama", founded on Hindoo mythology. His best prose-work is "The Life of Nelson". Southey was made Poet Laureate in 1813, and Wordsworth succeeded him to this dignity on his death.

— ·· —

XXIX. LORD BYRON.

MISS STEVENS. There were other poets, the contempories of the "Lake Poets", who also felt the crushing weight of artificial forms and needless tyranny, but they only looked at man's representation of God, in the current theology and rose in fierce revolt against God and man; they even threw off individual allegiance to duty and law. You know which great poet represents, in this way, the strong energy of revolt, and the bare assertion of self-will as the principles of life.

JANET. Byron "who looked on the world with bitterness and disgust". He was born in London in 1788. His father, Captain John Byron of the Guards, deserted his wife, Catherine Gordon of Gight, in a fit of dissipation, after having squandered most of her fortune. His mother returned to Aberdeen, when her little son, who was afflicted with lameness in one foot, was two years old.

MISS STEVENS. I am sorry to say Mrs. Byron was a capricious and violent woman, who could not teach self-control to the active and mischievous boy, so allowances must be made for the great poet, who rose against the restraints of society and law which in any way interfered with his own individual action. But go on, Edith, please.

EDITH. When Byron was eleven years old, his grand-uncle died, and he became a lord and the owner of Newstead Abbey in Nottinghamshire. He was sent to Harrow School to prepare for Cambridge, whither he went in 1805. He made some firm friends among the students, but greatly annoyed the college authorities by his irregular conduct.

MARY. I read somewhere that he not only kept bulldogs in his rooms, but also a bear cub, which he introduced to visitors as training for a fellowship; what irony!

MISS STEVENS. The young lord also neglected his studies, and eargerly devoured all kinds of books; especially those on Oriental History. But at the same time he made good use of his leisure hours. Which poems did he publish in 1807?

MARY. "The Hours of Idleness", which were severely dealt with by a writer in the "Edinburgh Review". The young poet retorted in a satirical poem entitled "English Bards and Scotch Reviewers", which showed that the pen could become a formidable and destructive weapon in his hand.

MISS STEVENS. He not only lashed his reviewer, Lord Brougham, but also men who had never harmed him, like Sir Walter Scott and Thomas Moore, the Irish poet who wrote the "Evening Bells" and the "Last Rose of Summer", and "Lalla Rookh, an Oriental Tale". He also attacked the Lakists, especially Southey, saying "God help thee, Southey, and thy readers too". After a little, he felt ashamed of himself, and tried to suppress the poem, but in vain. Where did he go to when he came of age?

FRANCES. He visited Spain and Turkey, a visit which inspired the first two cantos of "Childe Harold's Pilgrimage".

MISS STEVENS. In spite of his own repeated denials, we cannot help identifying the writer with this gloomy "Childe Harold", who had exhausted in revelry and vice the power of enjoying life. Yet what happened when his cantos were published?

MARY. Byron "awoke one morning and found himself famous". What a nice feeling that must be!

MISS STEVENS. The author who had been sneered at as a weakling only five years earlier, rose by unanimous consent to the head of the London literary world.

JANET. So he was the "literary lion" of the day! What a pity this happiness did not last!

MISS STEVENS. During the three last years it did, the poet wrote those fine Turkish tales, which kindled in the public mind of England an enthusiastic feeling towards modern Greece. Which are they?

FRANCES. "The Giaour", "The Bride of Abydos", "The Corsair" and "Lara", none of which I have ever read.

MISS STEVENS. In all four we find the inevitable, wasted and sallow Byronic hero again. "Childe Harold" has wound a crimson shawl round his high pale brow, and in full Greek dress, he glows on us with his melancholy eyes. Go on with his biography, please.

EDITH. In 1815 Byron married Miss Milbanke. Almost from the beginning there were disagreements, and in a twelve-month the union was dissolved. Byron left England, never more to return "to his native shore".

MISS STEVENS. The cause of the separation is even now a mystery. One daughter, Ada, to whom he addressed the touching lines which open the third canto of "Childe Harold", reminded the unhappy parents of what their home might have been. Where did he live abroad?

JANET. He travelled about a lonely wanderer over the blood-stained ground of Waterloo, (the "Eve of the Battle of Waterloo",) — amid the snowy summits of the Jura.

"The "Prisoner of Chillon") and in the beautiful land of Italy ("Italy").

MISS STEVENS. The faded palaces of Venice and the mouldering columns of Rome are fit emblems of the poet's ruined life. When did he finish "Childe Harold".

FRANCES. In 1818; the third Canto he wrote at Geneva, the fourth at Venice.

MISS STEVENS. The view of modern Rome; the starlight vision of the bleeding Gladiator, and the address to the Ocean, which no familiarity can rob of its sublime effect, are the finest passages of the closing Canto. Let us close Byron's life now.

FRANCES. He tried his pen at dramatic writing in "Cain", "Manfred", "Marino Faliero". These are his principal dramas. "The Corsair" is narrative. His last great literary effort was the composition of "Don Juan".

MISS STEVENS. Never were shining gold and black mire so industriously heaped together. It seems as if the unhappy bard, tired of hating his fellow-mortals, had turned with fierce mockery upon himself to degrade and trample on that very genius upon which was based his only claim to admiration. However, his last enterprise is the redeeming point of his life. Tell us about it, Mary.

MARY. Byron sympathised with the down-trodden Greeks, and worked hard for their independence. He joined the turbulent Suliotes and did much to calm them. But he died in his prime in 1824 at Missolonghi, the victim of a marsh fever.

MISS STEVENS. The body of the poet was brought to England, and interred in the family vault at Hucknall near Newstead.

MARY. I just remember that I learned some of the "Hebrew Melodies" with great enjoyment, when I was younger. I can still say "Jephtha's Daughter", "Saul", and "the Vision of Belshazzar".

EDITH. And I know "Fare thee well"; — he addressed it to his wife.

MISS STEVENS. This evening you may recite them both. I should like to mention another poet who, in his own way, expressed the spirit of revolt against tyranny, Percy Bysshe

Shelley. He was of all poets the most ideal. He longed to see man become at once good, great, and joyous, beautiful and free.

JANET. Shelley's life was very short. He was born in 1792, and in 1822 he was drowned by the upsetting of a boat in crossing the gulf of Spezzia.

MISS STEVENS. The finest of his poems is "Alastor, or the Spirit of Solitude", another is "Queen Mab". One of his last poems was "Adonis", a lament for another young poet, John Keats, to whom the world with all its evils could not be wholly dark.

MARY. It is he who says in "Endymion": "A thing of beauty is a joy for ever".

EDITH. His life was even shorter than Shelley's. He was born in 1796 and died in 1821 of consumption in Rome.

MISS STEVENS. Byron, Shelley and Keats are often called "the Post-Revolution Poets".

XXX. SIR WALTER SCOTT.

MISS STEVENS. We might have spoken of Sir Walter Scott, Wordsworth's dear friend, before, but I wanted to take him apart as he was not influenced by the French Revolution, as all the poets we have been speaking of lately were, but rather by the revival of literature, which was taking place in Germany.

MARY. I know which influence you mean, "the love for the free imagination of the old German ballads and legends".

EDITH. Our German governess told us a good deal about these romance writings of the "Romantic School" as she called it.

MISS STEVENS. We may call Sir Walter Scott a romance-writer in prose, if you like. What do you know of his life, Janet?

JANET. He was born in Edinburgh, on August 15 th 1771 just two years later than Napoleon I. When he was three years old, he became lame and, being unable to run about like other children, he amused himself by reading fairy-stories, old Scotch ballads, histories, and legends referring to the brave days of old.

MISS STEVENS. His imagination was constantly in exercise, and he lived in a very world of romance. If he saw an old castle or battle-field, he filled it at once with the living characters of the old world, and delighted his companions with stories of barons, knights and ladies of the days of chivalry. When he was quite a boy, he often lived with his grandfather in Roxburghshire, watching "the gentle ripple of the Tweed over its pebbles", so that with the Tweed above all other names, the memory of Scott is imperishably associated. But I interrupted you, go on, please.

JANET. His father, an attorney, was a Writer to the Signet and Scott was apprenticed to him; then he studied for the bar, and at the age of 21 he was called. But his heart was not in his profession. He was very thankful when his appointment as sheriff of Selkirkshire in 1799 gave him a fixed salary of £ 300 a year and plenty of leisure to devote himself to his favourite pursuits.

MISS STEVENS. His literary career had opened some years before with his Translations of Bürger's "Leonore" and the "Wild Huntsman"; capital translations as you know. In 1797 he had married a French lady, Charlotte Margaret Charpentier. Tell me which was his first important labour?

FRANCES. "The Minstrelsy of the Scottish Border" a collection of ballads, which he published in 1802.

MISS STEVENS. About that time Scott settled with his young wife at Ashestiel, a country-house on the Tweed. The house stood on a high and wooded bank, overlooking the river which, as I told you, he loved so well. Do you know his mode of life there and almost everywhere, Mary?

MARY. He rose at 5 o'clock, paid a visit to the stable to see his horses and dogs, returned to his study, worked with a dog or two at his feet till breakfast time, 9 or 10; according to his own words he had by that hour "broken the neck of the day's work." At 12 he was "his own man", — free for the day.

MISS STEVENS. You see that the French are right in saying "l'aurore est l'amie des Muses". Which poem raised Scott to a high place among the British poets, Edith?

EDITH. The "Lay of the Last Minstrel", which appeared in 1805. I think I like it nearly as much as "Marminon" or "A Tale of Flodden Field" — and the "Lady of the Lake", which followed soon.

MISS STEVENS. The popularity of these enchanting poems made the scenery of Scotland famous all over the world. What was the fair dream of the poet's life, Frances?

FRANCES. To become a Border "laird". When he had been promoted to the position of Clerk to the Court of Session with an income of £ 800 a year, he bought "a piece of land" on the Tweed and raised the grand Gothic mansion of Abbotsford, furnished it in the fashion of the feudal days, and lived in it like a knight of the olden times.

MISS STEVENS. Here he delighted to meet and entertain his friends, "singing ballads, and sounding the pibroch amidst the clinking of glasses, holding gay hunting parties, where yeoman and gentleman rode side by side, and encouraging lively dances, where the lord was not ashamed to give his hand to the miller's daughter". To keep up this grand style. Sir Walter, as he was now called, for he had received a baronetcy from the Government of the day, published first "Waverley", which appeared anonymously, and then one novel after another in quick succession. He even went into partnership with his publishers the Messrs. Ballantyne. You know what happened.

JANET. The firm failed and the author stood, at the age of 55, not only penniless, but burdened with a debt of £ 117,000. But this calamity brought out the noblest qualities of Scott's nature. Refusing to allow his creditors to suffer any loss that he could prevent, he devoted his life to the herculean task of removing this mountain of debt.

MISS STEVENS. Already his strong frame had been shaken by illness, yet the valiant soul was never shaken; even under the deep sorrow of his wife's death he worked on steadily and bravely, writing the "Life of Napoleon", "Woodstock", "Tales of a Grandfather" and several other works. Tell us about the close of his life, Mary, please.

6*

MARY. The toil was killing the poet; in 1830, he had a stroke of paralysis. His doctors sent him to Italy, but the visit did not do him any good. On his way home, the relentless malady struck him a mortal blow. His earnest wish was to die at Abbotsford within sight and sound of the Tweed. He recovered sufficiently to return to the well beloved place, and there he died, Sept. 21st 1832, surrounded by his family and with his favourite dog at his feet.

MISS STEVENS. You so often disagreed about which of his works is the best: "Ivanhoe", which revives the brilliant chivalrous days of Richard the Lion-hearted, or "The Talisman", which carries us to the East in the time of the 3rd crusade, or "Kenilworth", a picture of Elizabeth and her court, or "Quentin Durward", which introduces us to the French court during the reign of Louis XI, or "Guy Mannering", which tells us of life in the Lowlands and Highlands in times gone by, or "The Heart of Midlothian" or "Rob Roy", so that I won't touch upon the subject here for fear of raising an endless discussion. Let us say that all the 28 novels, called "the Waverley Novels", are of great interest by enabling us to enter into the feelings of persons living in ages remote from the present.

XXXI. THACKERAY.

MISS STEVENS. Sir Walter Scott used to say "that he had taught many ladies and gentlemen to write romances as well, or nearly as well as himself". On one occasion one of the guests at Abbotsford was decidedly one of these: Maria Edgeworth. Jane Austen was another lady novelist; George Eliot, the author of "Adam Bede", a third. But there are especially the two contemporaries, Thackeray and Dickens, who strove in their humorous novels to show how a society decays when it becomes insincere. Let us first speak of Thackeray.

FRANCES. William Makepeace Thackeray was born at Calcutta in 1811, where his father held an office in the Indian

Civil Service. At the age of seven, he was sent to England to the Charterhouse School. In 1829 he went up to Cambridge, but only for a year, for he had made up his mind to become an artist. In 1832 when he came of age, he came into the possession of an ample fortune.

MISS STEVENS. But it all passed through his hands in a year or two; part of it was lost at cards, part in an Indian bank, part in two unsuccessful newspapers. It was all the more trying for him as he had never learnt to draw accurately, and therefore could not become an artist. However, he turned his attention to literature as a means of support, and contributed many humorous tales and sketches to the periodicals, signing himself by all kinds of funny names. What papers did he contribute to Punch?

MARY. The "Snob" papers, and in 1840 he brought out the "Paris Sketch Book". I am looking forward, to reading his great novel "Vanity Fair" some day; what is it about, Miss Stevens?

MISS STEVENS. As I told you, the title indicates the vain high life of the upper ten, the hardening influence of money and dignity. The "Newcomes" is another popular novel, but the most perfect novel of Thackeray's is "Esmond", purporting to be an autobiography written in the time of Queen Anne. Which profession did Thackeray take up in 1851. Edith?

EDITH. He turned public lecturer choosing for his subject the English Humorists of the 18th century, and later on the four Georges.

MISS STEVENS. He delivered his lectures with great success both in England and America. His audience was chiefly composed of ladies. The lectures on the Georges contain some frightful pictures of court life. The character of the second George is described with bitter irony, while that of the fourth is held up to special ridicule and contempt. As the author was no historian, he may escape professional censure. When did the distinguished novelist die?

FRANCES. In 1859 he had started "the Cornhill Magazine" — he was still writing for it when his career was abruptly terminated. He died quite suddenly in 1863 in a house which he had lately built for himself at Palace Green.

XXXII. DICKENS.

MISS STEVENS. So at last we have come to Charles Dickens, who has afforded us already many opportunities for "a good laugh which is as good as a little medicine". Let us hear his biography.

JANET. He was born near Portsmouth in 1812. His early life was a very hard one. His father first held a situation in the Navy Pay Department, then he became a parliamentary reporter; later on he was imprisoned for having run into debt. Dickens often went to visit him, and in this way he met with the lowest classes of society.

MISS STEVENS. He gained experience which he afterwards turned to good account in his novels. The poor boy never had much schooling, for what education he got, he was mostly indebted to his own industry. To what occupation did he take after having been employed first in sticking labels on blacking bottles, and then as clerk in an attorney's office?

EDITH. He took to reporting, and proved himself shrewd and clever. During his leisure hours he rambled about the streets of London, remarking whatever was odd or humorous about the people, or peculiar about the places he saw.

MISS STEVENS. Under the name of "Boz", which his little sister first used in attempting to say "Moses", a nickname of one of Dickens' brothers, he published, in the "Morning Chronicle", several "Sketches". Which Papers followed?

MARY. The "Pickwick Papers", the amusing adventures of a party of Cockney sportsmen. They were "a hit" and the author's fame was established.

MISS STEVENS. Novel after novel followed from his ready pen, everything he wrote being eagerly welcomed by an enthusiastic and admiring public. Tell us in what order the novels were written, Edith.

EDITH. First came "Oliver Twist", the story of the poor orphan-boy who is brought up in the workhouse, then "Nicholas Nickleby", which exhibits the horrors of Dotheboys Hall and the brutal greed of Squeers, the low-bred schoolmaster.

MARY. It his he who says "it will be all the same a hundred years hence" when he starves and whips the boys. The horrid man!

EDITH. Then the "Old Curiosity Shop". a tale of an old gamester and his innocent grandchild, Little Nell.

MARY. When I first read the part about her death, I cried bitterly, as it is most touching.

MISS STEVENS. In 1842 Dickens paid a visit to America, where he received a hearty welcome. Do you know in which two books he dealt very severely with certain peculiarities of the Yankees. Janet?

JANET. In "American Notes for General Circulation" and "Martin Chuzzlewit", in which the renowned Mrs. Harris is made the authority for all the wonderful stories that Mrs. Sairey Gamp has to tell.

MISS STEVENS. Both books were very unpopular in America, and brought on their author a great amount of ill-will. Nevertheless the Americans continued to read and enjoy his books, and he gradually recovered their favour; as was proved on the occasion of his second visit to the United States in 1862. Which are his other books?

FRANCES. "David Copperfield", in the form of an autobiography, contains many of Dickens' own personal experiences; it was "the favourite child among the offspring of his genius", "Dombey and Son", a forerunner of Old Scrooge in the "Christmas Carol"; "Little Dorrit or Life in a Debtor's Prison", and the "Cricket on the Hearth".

MISS STEVENS. Dickens' charming series of Christmas stories took, in later years, the form of a Christmas number of "All the Year Round". The author took a journey to Italy, and wrote "Pictures from Italy", but he longed to get back again to the London streets and crowds, in which, according to his own words, he felt happiest. Where did he spend the closing years of his life?

JANET. In 1856 he purchased the house at Gad's Hill, near Rochester, which he had often admired twenty-five years previously. He often came up to London for Readings out of his own novels, to which people flocked, for he was a brilliant reader. He died on June 9ᵗʰ 1870, while sitting at his desk.

He was buried in Westminster Abbey.

XXXIII. MACAULAY.

MISS STEVENS. In the domain of history, the activity of the 19ᵗʰ century has been immense. A new standard of exact research, that is to say of the comparing and testing of many kinds of evidence has been developed. Macaulay has succeeded in making history interesting to a degree never attempted before, and Carlyle has turned a light of often startling brilliancy upon the scenes and characters of the past. What do you know of the former, Janet?

JANET. Thomas Babington Macaulay was born at Rothley Temple in Leicestershire in 1800. He was of Scotch origin, his grandfather having been a Presbyterian minister. His father was a London merchant and philanthropist; he was the friend of Canon Wilberforce who exerted himself so much for the abolition of slavery. Macaulay was an extraordinarily precocious child. Before he was 8 years old, he wrote not only Ballads and Hymns, but also History. He had a marvellous memory too.

MISS STEVENS. Once, when only a boy of 6, he picked up a copy of the "Lay of the Last Minstrel" at a friend's house, where his father had taken him to call. He read a few pages, and, when he came home, he repeated to his mother stanza after stanza, till she was tired of listening.

MARY. I wish I had a little bit of his memory, then I could repeat "the Battle of Ivry" by this wonderful man better than I do, or some of the "Lays of Ancient Rome".

MISS STEVENS. From his 13ᵗʰ to his 18ᵗʰ year, he attended a private school. At that time his rapidity in learning was the wonder and envy of his companions. But, as he grew older, he paid less attention to class-room work, and more to general reading, for which his keen appetite could never be satisfied. To which university did he go, Edith?

EDITH. To Cambridge, where he twice gained the Chancellor's gold medal for English poetry. In the Union Debating Society, he won great distinction too. During his undergraduate years, he was a contributor to several Magazines. While preparing for the bar, he achieved his first literary triumph with his brilliant essay "On Milton" which appeared in the "Edinburgh Review". Soon after, Macaulay became a barrister, but literature and politics had stronger attractions for him than his profession. In 1830 he entered the House of Commons, first as M. P. for Calne in Wiltshire, then for Leeds.

MISS STEVENS. He was first made a Commissioner of the Board of Control and then its Secretary. At that time he worked very hard in contributing brilliant articles to the "Edinburgh Review", but, with all his hard work, he could not earn enough to support both himself and his sisters, who were now dependent on him. What position did he therefore gladly accept, Mary?

MARY. In return for his services to his party, he was appointed to a government office, a seat on the Supreme Council of India, at Calcutta, in 1834.

MISS STEVENS. As President of the Committee on Public Instruction, Macaulay rendered an important service to India as well as to England, for it was by his advice that the English tongue was adopted as the medium for educating the natives. He rendered valuable service too by his large share in the composition of the Indian Penal Code. Which two "Essays" did the author write after his return in 1838?

JANET. Those on "Clive" and "Warren" Hastings, which were the result of his study of Indian history.

MISS STEVENS. Soon after his return, he was elected member for Edinburgh. He held successively the offices of Secretary of War and Paymaster-General of the Forces. In 1847 he displeased his supporters or constituents and, in a pet, they rejected him; but in 1852 they re-elected him of their own accord. Which great work had been begun in the interval?

FRANCES. "The History of England from the Accession of James II"; the success of the first two volumes, issued in November 1848, was such as never had been known before.

MISS STEVENS. The plan of the work was a great one; Macaulay said: "I purpose to write the history of England from the accession of King James II down to a time which is within the memory of men still living." The great historian who depicted the events of the past in such a fresh and striking colouring, did not live to complete his design. The narrative was brought down to the death of William III only, that means a period of a little more than 15 years. Macaulay, with his wonderful memory, was able to collect and retain stores of information from all manner of old books, papers and parchments, and to give life-like portraits of the great men of the age. He also excelled in descriptions of landscapes and street scenes, spirit-stirring insurrections, trials and sieges. Do you remember which extracts we read last winter?

JANET. The Battle of Sedgemoor between the Duke of Monmouth and the Royalist army under Lord Churchill; also the Execution of Monmouth.

EDITH. I liked the chapter on William the Third's youth so much; it reads just like a novel.

FRANCES. I enjoyed the description of the Country-Gentlemen of the 17th century, although I think Macaulay does not quite do justice to that time.

MISS STEVENS. The great historian is not always impartial; his English is pure and vigorous, but deficient in the highest qualities of English prose. Mary mentioned his splendid poems. When did he die?

MARY. In 1859, quite suddenly of heart-disease, after having been created baron of Rothley in 1857 in consideration of his great literary merit. He was buried in Westminster Abbey.

XXXIV. CARLYLE.

MISS STEVENS. Thomas Carlyle was a Scotchman too, but his mind was so thoroughly steeped in German authors that both his thought and style were influenced by them. What do you remember about his life, Edith?

EDITH. He was born in 1795 in Dumfriesshire. As he showed remarkable powers of mind, his father, a mason and builder, of strong intellect and deep religious feeling, resolved to educate him for the Scottish Church. At the early age of 14, Carlyle passed to the University of Edinburgh, where he devoted himself chiefly to the study of mathematics.

MISS STEVENS. After leaving the university, he was a private tutor for some time, but soon he found out that teaching was not his proper calling. He was drawn to literature with a power which he could not resist. Which was his first literary effort, Mary?

MARY. Several short biographies on "Montaigne", "Nelson" and the "Two Pitts". Then he published a translation of Goethe's "Wilhelm Meister". This was followed by a "Life of Schiller" in the London Magazine.

MISS STEVENS. After this, he settled in London. He had married Jane Baillie Welsh, who had made up her mind to marry a man of genius and who, as some one said, "received what she had bargained for to the uttermost farthing". Where did they live before going to London? .

FRANCES. At Craigenputtoch, in the midst of the black moors of Dumfriesshire, I should say near "the wilds of Galloway", if I were not afraid of hurting Janet's feelings.

MISS STEVENS. The sojourn in the desert of Craigenputtoch suited the literary hermit bent on work, but it was misery to his wife who was fond of society. She was forced to drudge at housekeeping while her husband was engaged at his literary work, and she did it without complaining.

What was the result of the Craigenputtoch exile, Janet?

JANET. "Sartor Resartus" ("the Patcher Repatched"). I have often seen the book with the picture in the frontispice at home, but I never read it.

MISS STEVENS. It purports to be a review of a German work on dress; in it, Carlyle inveighs against the old clothes of falsehood and fiction, that conceal the divine idea lying at the centre of human life, so it is in reality a philosophical essay. But at length Carlyle wearied of his desert life, especially when the want of books hampered his work. He removed with his wife, whose health was impaired, to Chelsea. Which great work did he begin at once there?

EDITH. The "French Revolution", a History. I read that the manuscript of the first volume was accidentally destroyed by his great friend, John Stuart Mill, the philosopher, who was to have made suggestions on it, but that Carlyle uttered no reproach and set to work to rewrite the lost volume.

MISS STEVENS. The work was written as neither history, nor English had ever been written before, in consequence it was not at once successful, but by and by its great merits were recognized, and its author's place in the front rank of literature was assured. What did Carlyle do after the publication of this great work, Mary?

MARY. He delivered lectures on "German Literature", the "History of Literature", "Heroes and Hero-Worship", and so on. I should like to read Carlyle's last great work, "The History of Frederick the Great" that must be interesting!

MISS STEVENS. The author did not profess to set up Frederick as a hero to be worshipped, but he found him honest beyond the standard of his generation. "He managed not to be a liar and a charlatan as his century was." He began to write the book in 1851, and completed it in 1865; in the same year a great honour was conferred on him.

EDITH. He was elected Lord Rector of Edinburgh University. When he was delivering his inaugural address in that city, his wife died suddenly in her carriage in Hyde Park.

MISS STEVENS. His grief was great; and he never wholly recovered from it. He occupied his later years in preparing his wife's "Letters and Memorials" and in writing "Reminiscences" of his own life. He died in 1881 and was buried by his own desire in the kirkyard of Ecclefechan by the side of his parents. Thomas de Quincey, the author of "Confessions of an Opium Eater" has often been placed on a par with Carlyle as a Master of English prose.

XXXV. MODERN NOVELISTS.

MISS STEVENS. We might speak of the other prose-writers of our day before we speak of the poets. What do you know of Bulwer, Lord Lytton?

JANET. He was the youngest son of General Bulwer of Haydon Hall, Norfolk, and was born in 1805. He received a careful education from his talented mother, to whose estate he succeeded, and whose name he took. His first book was published when he was 15.

MARY. Another prodigy like Pope and Macaulay!

MISS STEVENS. At Cambridge he won the Chancellor's Medal for his poem "Sculpture". Before he settled down to a life of hard literary toil, he travelled on foot over England and Scotland, and afterwards visited France on horseback. Please finish his life, Edith.

EDITH. In 1838, on the occasion of her Majesty's coronation, he was created a baronet, and in 1866 he was raised to the peerage as Baron Lytton. He was an M. P. for many years and was distinguished for his powers as an orator. He died in 1873.

MISS STEVENS. Of the multitude of his works, it may be said, that while his earlier productions are tainted with the worst faults of Byron, his later writings are more healthy in tone and superior in every way. He published poems, dramas, metrical translations of foreign authors, novels, essays, histories and political pamphlets; but his fame rests chiefly on his abilities as a novelist. In the novels he has chosen his subjects from Italy and Greece, from France and Germany, from the England of the Past and the England of the Present, from high life, low life, and country life. We read his three best novels together.

FRANCES. "Rienzi", "the Last Days of Pompei", and the "Last of the Barons".

MISS STEVENS. Later on you may read "Night and Morning". "Eugene Aram", the "Caxtons", a family picture, and "My Novel" or "Varieties of English Life". Some years ago we acted one of his comedies, "Money", which is very amusing.

Of Captain Marryat's life, there is not much to say; he was always at sea.

MARY. "Jacob Faithful", "Frank Mildmay", "Midshipman Easy", and "Peter Simple", are just as much liked by schoolboys as the "Last of the Mohicans" and the "Spy", both by Fennimore Cooper.

MISS STEVENS. You all read that splendid biography of Charles Kingsley in our library. Tell us what you remember about it.

FRANCES. He was the son of a Devonshire clergyman and was born in 1819. He went to Cambridge, and then entered the Church. He soon became Rector of Eversley, a moorland parish in Hampshire. Kingsley was very much beloved by his parishioners, but he had to leave them. He was for some time Professor of Modern History at Cambridge. In 1859 the Queen made him one of her chaplains, as she liked him very much. He took an active part in all the socialistic movements of the working classes. He was a popular man. Kingsley died in 1875.

MISS STEVENS. You all read "Westward Ho!" founded on Elizabethan sailor life. I shall let you have "Hypatia", the story of the celebrated Alexandrian philosopher. Later on you may read "Yeast", and "Two years Ago". — To finish the novelists, we will speak of Washington Irving, the American Goldsmith. Who has a great liking for him?

MARY. I enjoyed reading the "Sketchbook" and the "Tales of the Alhambra" very much. He was born in New York in 1783, but he was really Scotch. His father was partner in a firm in Liverpool, which was confided to his care.

When the firm failed, Irving turned author by profession.

MISS STEVENS. This was up-hill work at first, but Sir Walter Scott encouraged the young author, whose style became so charming, whatever his subject was an English: Manor House with bright fires and Christmas snow, a drowsy Scotch farm, a steading in Sleepy Hollow (Rip van Winkle), a moon-lit court in the Alhambra — the great Italian sailor (Life of Columbus), the sweet-souled Irish author (Life of Goldsmith), the noble American General (Life of Washington) that it fascinates us by the poetic graces of his fancy. Where did he spend the eve of his life?

EDITH. At Sunnyside, a pleasant seat by the Hudson. He died there in 1859.

XXXVI. LONGFELLOW.

MISS STEVENS. America not only produced an excellent prose-writer, but also a poet of considerable eminence, of whose poetry it has been said "That it is a gospel of goodwill, set to music", as it has carried "sweetness and light" to thousands of homes.

JANET. That is my favourite poet, Henry Wadsworth Longfellow who was born at Portland, Maine, in 1807. He speaks of his native town in "My Lost Youth", as "the beautiful town, that is seated by the sea". At the early age of 14, Longfellow entered Bowdoin College, at Brunswick. Here he revealed his poetical bent in several short poems contributed to "The United States Literary Gazette". After graduating with honours in 1825, at the age of 18, he remained at Bowdoin as tutor, and at the age of nineteen he was offered the Professorship of Modern Languages.

MARY. He was a young professor, dear me!

MISS STEVENS. After his appointment, he received the customary leave of absence; he spent three years and a half in France, Italy, Spain, Germany, Holland and England. As in the case of Washington Irving his contact with the old world widened his sympathies, and prevented him from being purely an American author. Go on, Frances.

FRANCES. He returned to America in 1829, and entered on his professorial duties with enthusiasm. In 1831 he married Mary Potter. He wrote articles in the "North American Review", and he published notes of travel under the title of "Outre-Mer".

MISS STEVENS. As early as 1834, he was elected Professor of Modern Languages in the University of Harvard, the foremost seat of learning in America. That involved another period of European travel. In the midst of it, a great sorrow cast its shadow on his young life.

JANET. His wife died at Rotterdam; how very sad!

MISS STEVENS. On his return he wrote his romance of "Hyperion", and, in the same year, he gave the world his first volumes of poems.

EDITH. "Voices of the Night". It contains lovely poems such, as: "The Reaper and the Flowers" and the "Psalm of Life".

MISS STEVENS. Two years later, another volume of Ballads and other Poems established his fame. Which poems do they include, Mary?

MARY. "The Wreck of the Hesperus", which I always confused with "Casabianca", by Mrs. Hemans, when I was younger — "Excelsior" and the "Village Blacksmith".

MISS STEVENS. Longfellow paid a third visit to Europe in 1842; it is chiefly memorable on account of the "Poems of Slavery", which he wrote on board ship during the homeward voyage.

Not long after his return, he married his second wife, Frances Appleton. They settled in his house at Harvard, which all Americans regard with feelings of reverence.

JANET. How I should love to see it, but I fear I never shall. He worked very hard in it, for he wrote "The Spanish Student", the "Poets of Europe", another volume of poems entitled "The Belfry of Bruges", "Evangeline" and the "Golden Legend", a mystery play.

MISS STEVENS. In 1854 he resigned his professorship, and, a year later, he published the quaint "Indian Edda", as it has been called, or epic "Hiawatha", which was followed by the "Courtship of Miles Standish", and by "Birds of

Passage" including "My Lost Youth" which Janet told us
about. In 1861 he had to encounter another great sorrow.
EDITH. The tragic death of his second wife, who was
burned in his house at Harvard.
MISS STEVENS. That second overwhelming trial chastened
his spirit, but did not extinguish his poetic powers. In work
he found refuge from his sorrow, and by and by he gave the
world his "Tales of a Wayside Inn" and his translation of
the "Divina Commedia" of Dante. Tell us what great honours
were about this time bestowed on the poet?
FRANCES. In 1868 he received from Cambridge the degree
of LL. D. and in the following year he visited England again
and was made a D. C. L. of Oxford. He died at Harvard
on March 24ᵗʰ 1882.

XXXVII. TENNYSON.

MISS STEVENS. We can continue our Talks with a poet,
who not only wrote ballads and epic poems, but also lyrics
and philosophical elegies. He mastered the English tongue
and verse in a wonderful way, and he well deserved to wear
the wreath as Poet-Laureate for more than 40 years. His
life is rather uneventful; tell us about it, Mary.
MARY. Alfred Tennyson was the youngest son of a
Lincolnshire clergyman; he was sent to Cambridge, where he
won the Chancellor's Medal for a poem in English blank
verse, "Timbuctoo". About the same time, he joined his
brother Charles in the publication of "Poems by two brothers".
In 1830 appeared a volume entitled "Poems, Chiefly Lyrical"
by Alfred Tennyson, but the public did not seem to care
for them.
MISS STEVENS. Undaunted by the frigid reception of this
first venture, Tennyson published a second volume in 1833,
containing, besides corrected reprints of some former poems,
"The Miller's daughter", "The Lotos Eaters", and above all
"The Queen of the May", an exquisitely touching picture of a

pretty village girl fading away amid the brightening blossoms of an English spring.

Still the critics were unkind and unjust to the youthful singer, and for 9 years the sweet voice was silenced. But it was not the silence of an idle life; "Locksley Hall", "Lady Clara Vere de Vere", "Morte d'Arthur", and "Godiva" were in preparation. When they appeared in 1842, the victory was won. When did he publish his next work, Janet?

JANET. In 1847, "The Princess, a Medley". Seven college men tell the tale of the prince and princess who are betrothed without having met. It is at the same time a playful satire on the claim of women to enjoy the same education as men.

MISS STEVENS. Early in life a great sorrow had fallen on Tennyson: Arthur Henry Hallam who had been the poet's bosom friend died at college in Vienna. In 1850 Tennyson published "In Memoriam", in which we find the lines so often quoted:

> "I hold it true whate'er befall,
> I feel it when I sorrow most,
> 'Tis better to have loved and lost,
> Than never to have loved at all".

What happened in the same year?

FRANCES. Tennyson was made Poet Laureate on the death of Wordsworth.

MISS STEVENS. In 1855 "Maud" and other Poems appeared, and in 1859 the "Idylls of the King", forming the first part of an epic, of which King Arthur is the hero, undoubtedly his greatest work. What other poem appeared later on?

MARY. "Enoch Arden", a very touching story, which I can hadly believe to be true, though it is said to be true.

MISS STEVENS. Tennyson's poetry is pure, tender and ennobling; it has great power to work on the emotions. He did much to battle with that tendency to the common-place and matter-of-fact ideas which is characteristic of our money-getting age. His life was a quiet one. As you know, he lived latterly at Farringford in the Isle of Wight, seeing no society, but a few chosen friends. He died in 1892 after a short illness, and was buried in Westminster Abbey.

I should like you to remember that well-known line of his,

"'Tis only noble to be good".

If you carry it out in life you will surely be happy.

—   —

XXXVIII. ROBERT BROWNING.

MISS STEVENS. Tennyson and Browning have been compared and contrasted as often as Dickens and Thackeray. The two poets differ as much in their aims and their styles as the two novelists. What are the chief features of Tennyson's poetry?

JANET. Beauty and sweetness, I think.

MISS STEVENS. You are right; those of Browning's poetry are ruggedness and strength. Tennyson's thought is profuse but clear; Browning is condensed to a fault. Browning's life was as uneventful as Tennyson's. Begin telling us about it, Edith.

EDITH. Robert Browning was born at Camberwell in Surrey in 1812; he was educated at the University of London. In 1841 the poet went to Italy, where he resided for a few years.

MISS STEVENS. The study of Italian history, literature and art coloured all his later works. His first important work, "Paracelsus", published in 1836, is a deeply thoughtful poem, which was praised by a few cultivated readers, but most persons were puzzled by its obscurity. One of the first fruits of the Italian study was another most puzzling poem "Sordello".

MARY. I read that a critic once said of that poem: "I have read "Sordello"; and there are only two lines in the volume which are intelligible, the first and the last."

MISS STEVENS. Browning turned to the Drama as affording the best medium for the exhibition and working out of character. Who knows the names of some of his plays?

FRANCES. "Pippa Passes". Pippa is a factory girl, who

7*

passes the chief persons of the drama at critical moments, and thus exercises an influence on their fates.

EDITH. "A Blot on the Scutcheon" which was brought out at Drury Lane in 1843.

MISS STEVENS. The latter is considered the best of the author's dramas. Another that possesses great merit is "King Victor and King Charles". Do you know whom Browning married in 1846?

MARY. Elizabeth Barrett, the well-known poetess of "The Cry of the Children".

MISS STEVENS. The poet-couple lived in Florence, till the death of Mrs. Browning in 1861. Which is the work that secured for Browning general recognition as a leading poet, Janet?

JANET. "Men and Women", published in 1855.

MISS STEVENS. Some of his ballads are full of spirit, and also free from that obscurity, which repels readers from his greater poems. Which of them do you know, Edith?

EDITH. "The Pied Piper of Hamelin", quite a true ballad, a song that tells a story. The same subject has been treated by a German poet Julius Wolff and even set to music in an opera.

FRANCES. I read "Heroé Riel", the Breton Sailor, who saved the retreating French fleet after the Battle of La Hogue in 1692; and the "Good News from Ghent".

MISS STEVENS. The most elaborate of all Browning's poems is "The Ring and the Book", the story of a Roman murder, told in ten different soliloquies by the leading actors of the drama. Do you know the titles of his later works Janet?

JANET. "The Inn Album", "Evelyn Hope", "The Twins", which has been called "Give and it shall be given unto you".

MISS STEVENS. The subject of this poem is taken from the Table Talk of Martin Luther. There are other poems which you will still have to read, as "La Saisiaz", "The two Poets", "Croisic" and "Filine at the Fair". There are all marked by masculine strength, keen insight into character, and marvellous power of condensed expression.

MISS STEVENS. Browning was an Honorary Fellow of Balliol College, Oxford, and, in former years, we often saw him here. When did he die, Mary?

MARY. In 1889 at Venice.

MISS STEVENS. Browning's readers and admirers have greatly increased in recent years, and "Browning Clubs" for the study of the poet's works have been formed in several cities.

XXXIX. RUSKIN.

MISS STEVENS. John Ruskin is the greatest of art critics. No one has ever written with greater eloquence and power about pictures and artists, about landscapes and architecture, and about the beauty and the grandeur of Nature, which the artist seeks to reproduce. When was he born, Frances?

FRANCES. He was born in 1819 in London, where his father, a native of Perth, was a wealthy wine-merchant. Ruskin was an only child, and from the time he was 5 years of age, his father used to take him, as well as his mother, on his annual journey over England, Wales, or Scotland.

MISS STEVENS. He also travelled abroad at an unusually early age. He brought back with him distinct and memorable impressions of all he had seen.

MARY. What a lucky child he was! But for all that luck, I should not like to be an only child, for it must be dull!

MISS STEVENS. His earliest teachers, after he had passed the stage of nursery tales, were Walter Scott and Pope in his translation of the "Iliad".

On Sundays he read the "Pilgrim's Progress" and "Robinson Crusoe". These were his own choice. His mother, who carried on his early education, required him to read through the Bible once a year.

MARY. I presume (I suppose) Ruskin was a precocious child, wasn't he?

MISS STEVENS. Indeed he was; he began to write stories and verses in his seventh year, and, at nine, he wrote an elaborate poem "On the Universe". He was very fond of drawing; his father, one of Turner's most devoted admirers, encouraged him in his fondness.

MARY. When did this little artist go to school?

MISS STEVENS. Not till he was fourteen, and then his girlish manners exposed him to a great deal of banter, but he was sustained by what he calls "the fountain of pure conceit" in his heart. When did he make his first essays in authorship, Edith?

EDITH. In 1836, when he was seventeen; they consisted of some boyish productions in a volume entitled "Friendship's Offering". In the same year, he wrote a reply to an attack on Turner whose pictures he greatly admired. He sent the manuscript to Turner for his approval, but the painter thought it best that no notice should be taken of the attack upon him. Hence the first chapter of "Modern Painters" did not as yet see the light.

MISS STEVENS. Ruskin came to Christ Church as a gentleman commoner. His mother occupied lodgings in the town through all the time of his residence here, in order to be near her son.

FRANCES. Did he distinguish himself in his studies?

MISS STEVENS. Not greatly. He, however, gained the "Newdegate" prize for English poetry in 1837. What happened the year after?

JANET. In 1838, he came of age, and on his birthday, his father informed him that stock had been transferred to his name, which would yield him an income of £ 200 a year.

MISS STEVENS. One of the first purchases he made with his money was that of Turner's "Harlech" for which he paid 70 guineas. He was nervous about his final examination, and worked very hard, so that he brought on a sharp attack of lung disease.

MARY. Another warning to you, friends, who wish to pass the Higher Women. Did he give up the thought of taking a degree?

MISS STEVENS. No, he put off his graduation till 1842. In the interval, he made the personal acquaintance of Turner.

JANET. It must have been a great pleasure to him, for he was a firm believer in Turner's art, and he has spent a great part of his life in explaining the splendid artist's principles.

MISS STEVENS. The remainder of Ruskin's life is little more than the record of his numerous books. When was the first volume of his greatest work, "Modern Painters", published?

FRANCES. In 1843; he signed it only "A Graduate of Oxford"; the book made a great impression on account of its deep thought, its elegance of style, and its pure English.

MISS STEVENS. In the interval between the issue of the second and third volumes, Ruskin wrote two other great works: "The Seven Lamps of Architecture" and "The Stones of Venice".

JANET. I read an extract from the first, and I found a description of a scene in the Alps most beautiful.

MISS STEVENS. Ruskin's writing is both beautiful and powerful. As an interpreter of the aspects of nature, he is almost unrivalled. What lectures did he deliver, Frances?

FRANCES. In 1861, Ruskin was elected Rede Lecturer at Cambridge and, in 1872, he was elected Slade Professor Lecturer of fine Arts at Oxford.

MISS STEVENS. His "Lectures on Art" have produced distinct effects on English art. They have led to the cultivation of a more earnest spirit, especially in the younger race of artists; some of these formed a society or school, called the "Pre-Raphaelite". Their leading principle is truth to Nature, so that the artist should paint either what he sees, or what he considers might have been the actual facts of the scene he desires to represent.

XL. CONCLUDING CHAPTER.

MISS STEVENS. We have come to the concluding chapter of the Victorian Age. In the category of Poet Painters of the "Pre-Raphaelite School", stands the founder Rossetti. When was he born, Edith?

EDITH. Dante Gabriel Rossetti was born in London in 1828. His father was the well-known Italian patriot and Dante scholar. It was always understood in the family that Gabriel should be a painter, as his artistic instinct seems to have shown itself very early.

MISS STEVENS. On the other hand, it is stated that at the age of five he wrote a sort of play, called "The Slave". One of his most masterly efforts was written as early as 1846, "The Blessed Damozel", and in 1848 he wrote a short prose story of a mystic kind, entitled "Hand and Soul". The external incidents of Rossetti's life are few. He was averse to exhibiting his pictures, so they remained unknown to the public at large. His "Poems" and his "Sonnets" are full of Italian tenderness, and a mystical yearning for the ideal. The same sympathies existed in his friends William Morris and Swinburne. Where did Rossetti die, Frances?

FRANCES. In his picturesque old house in Cheyne Walk, Chelsea, in 1882, where he had almost led the life of a recluse.

MISS STEVENS. He belonged to a singularly gifted family. His brother, William Michael, translated the "Inferno" into English blank-verse; his sister Christina is a true poetess. Do you know any other Women Poets of our age, Janet?

JANET. Felicia Hemans and Adelaide Procter.

MISS STEVENS. Both of them wrote beautiful poems, pervaded by the spirit of faith, hope and charity.

MARY. We learned "The Better Land", "Casabianca", and "The Homes of England" by Mrs. Hemans.

FRANCES. I learned "The Message" by Miss Procter.

JANET. I read "The Goblin Market" by Christina Rossetti.

MISS STEVENS. America has produced another sympathetic poet, whom one of you may have read.

JANET. James Russel Lowell. I read his "Selected Poems" with his "Message", — and how it helped me!

MISS STEVENS. Whose son was the poet Matthew Arnold, Edith?

EDITH. He was the son of Dr. Arnold of Rugby, who was the determined opponent of the Oxford movement, headed by Cardinal Newman.

MISS STEVENS. Matthew Arnold was born in 1822; he was both a prose-writer and a poet. He has an intellectual love for the good, beautiful and true, but he often makes only a vague impression on us. Which of his poems did you learn, Mary?

MARY. "Philomela" with the closing lines: "Eternal Passion, Eternal Pain!"

MISS STEVENS. I will mention Sir Edwin Arnold, whose "Raja Ride" we read. Who is the present Poet Laureate, Janet?

JANET. Alfred Austin; he was born in 1835. I read "The Death of Huss", "In the month when sings the Cuckoo", "Ave Maria".

MISS STEVENS. "Savonarola" is another of his poems. His "Poetry of the Period" justly attracted notice, although he bore down mercilessly upon the "feminine, narrow, domesticated, timorous" verse of the day. Who is the most popular and original poet of the present time? I might even say, the patriotic poet of the British Empire in its widest sense?

FRANCES. Rudyard Kipling, born in 1865.

MISS STEVENS. I have brought a copy of "The God of Things As They Are", and I will read you "L'Envoi" from "The Seven Seas", which will form a worthy conclusion of our Talks.

When Earth's last picture is painted and the tubes are
        twisted and dried,
When the oldest colours have faded, and the youngest
        critic has died,
We shall rest, and faith we shall need it — lie down for
        an aeon or two,
Till the Master of All Good Workmen shall put us to
        work anew!

And those that were good shall be happy; they shall sit
in a golden chair;
They shall splash at a ten-league canvas with brushes of
comet's hair;
They shall find real saints to draw from — Magdalene,
Peter and Paul;
They shall work for an age at a sitting and never be
tired at all!
And only the Master shall praise us and only the Master
shall blame;
And no one shall work for money, and no one shall work
for fame,
But each for the joy of the working and each in his
separate star,
Shall draw the Thing as he sees It for the God of Things
as they are.

I.

A Modern Play

or

English Proverbs

in three Acts.

✧

Persons.

Mrs. GORDON.
Mrs. CUMMING.
Miss (NELLY) GORDON.
Miss LILY GORDON.
Miss (KATE) CUMMING.
Miss ALICE CUMMING.
A housemaid.

ACT I.

SCENE I

Mrs. GORDON and Miss LILY GORDON are sitting in the drawing-room (an English drawing-room with couch, rocking-chairs, and a piano in the middle of the room); Mrs. GORDON is doing some sewing, whilst LILY is painting.

LILY. I wonder when Nellie will come home to-day, — she never tires of going round in the parish talking to old people and cheering the sick.

MRS. GORDON. I am glad she loves visiting the poor and infirm.

LILY. I know you do, mother dear.

MRS. GORDON. You see this dear child has found out by happy experience that *the way to be happy is to make others happy.*

LILY. I quite believe this is the secret to make life bright — especially when I think of Kate and Alice Cumming. They only please themselves, and whenever I see them, they complain of feeling dull.

MRS. GORDON. I am truly sorry for these girls. I should so like to make Mrs. Cumming see that she brings up her girls in the wrong way.

LILY. Dearest mother, that will be quite impossible. As you say yourself, *Every crow thinks her chickens the whitest;* Mrs. Cumming is more than satisfied with her daughters.

MRS. GORDON. Yes, the proverb is right: *There are none so blind as those who won't see.*

LILY. Therefore do give up talking to your friend about her wrong ideas.

MRS. GORDON. No child; I consider it my duty to tell her she is wrong in letting her daughters waste so much precious time.

LILY. Well, mother, if I ventured to advise you again, I might quote the school-boys' favourite proverb: *Don't teach your grandmother to suck eggs.* Of course you know better than I do, but I am sorry you *waste your breath* or rather that *you beat the air* in lecturing your friend.

MRS. GORDON. I hope I don't, child. You see life is so uncertain, "to-day man puts forth the tender leaves of hope, to-morrow blossoms, the third day comes a frost, a killing frost".

LILY. Mother dear, did you always speak in proverbs or quote Shakespeare or some other poet? I think you are quite marvellous.

MRS. GORDON. There is nothing marvellous about it; I like to recall all the passages of my favourite authors or some common proverb; they may make a lasting impression on your mind.

LILY. Depend upon it, Mother darling, we shall never forget what you have taught us, and especially we shall always thank you for having brought us up so well, so that we learnt the value of time.

MRS. GORDON. *Time is money,* the Englishman says, but ah! sometimes it is more than money.

LILY. And *Lost time is never found again.*

MRS. GORDON. To be sure, you are quite right, but pray, child, don't joke, but take it in earnest.

LILY. I am not joking! I think *I practise what I preach,* for I have been working very hard, I have not wasted one minute since luncheon time, and now my copy is finished.

MRS. GORDON. Let me see it, darling (Lily shows the painting to her mother). You have done it very nicely; I am thankful to think you will always be able to make your own living, should you be obliged to.

LILY. At any rate I would try to. I should then *put my pride into my pocket,* and make designs for a shop, if I found no higher work.

MRS. GORDON. There's a good girl! but *enough is as good as a feast;* you had better stop now. Go and see if your sister is coming.

LILY. I will *do as I am bid.* May I leave my brush, pallet etc. on the low chair here?

MRS. GORDON. I had rather you would take them to the proper place. *A place for everything, and everything in its right place* is as true as *A stitch in time saves nine.* I expect our friend will call, I have not seen her for a long time.

LILY. Are any of the girls coming with her? If so, I should like to stay.

MRS. GORDON. I don't know; but if I am not mistaken, I hear some one coming up the Avenue. Go and look if it is Mrs. Cumming.

LILY (going to the window). Yes, it is she, ringing the front-door bell, but without her sweet daughters, so I can go out by the back door and join Nell. (Exit.)

Scene II.

The parlour maid shows in Mrs. CUMMING, who enters the room grandly dressed. Mrs. GORDON goes to the door to meet her; they shake hands.

MRS. GORDON. How are you? I am so glad to see you again.

MRS. CUMMING. Thank you; how are you? It seems ages since we last met. We have had so many engagements; the girls have been twice to London at Drury-Lane and the Hay-Market; they had several invitations to picnics on the river too. Boating is so delightful and healthy an amusement for young people. How are you getting on? Working and plodding all the day and living *solitary as an oyster?*

MRS. GORDON. Thank you. *The trivial round, the common task* is not dull for us. I like my daughters to know the value of each moment, for *time is fleeting fast.*

MRS. CUMMING. My dear Mrs. Gordon, allow me to tell you that it is quite ridiculous to bring up your daughters in such a "bourgeois" way. I never knew any one like you. You treat them exactly like school-girls; they have always *to be up to time* and work like clockwork. Why won't you let them enjoy themselves as long as they are young?

MRS. GORDON. My dear Mrs. Cumming, *there is no accounting for tastes,* says the proverb. I do not at all agree with you. I hold that Jeremiah is right in saying: "It is good for a man that he bear the yoke in his youth".

MRS. CUMMING. You even quote this old prophet — very well, let a man bear it then, altho' if I had any sons, I should not be "*Old Mrs. Grundy*" and frown at them constantly; but do let a young woman enjoy herself. You make your girls work as if they had to earn their living.

MRS. GORDON. Well, who knows whether they may not be obliged to, some day. Nowadays life is such a struggle that one should be prepared for all eventualities; women as well as men.

MRS. CUMMING. But your daughters are provided for. Colonel Gordon left a nice fortune.

MRS. GORDON. *Fortunes may be lost;* you read of breaking of Banks almost every day. Education is the only fortune which can never be lost when once acquired.

MRS. CUMMING. My dear friend — you are a philosopher. Higher Education is all very well — for middle-class girls, but not for the daughters of gentlemen.

MRS. GORDON. You reproached me just now for being old-fashioned. I take the liberty of telling you now that you are *much behind the time.* Education is the privilege of every class of society. Work is honourable to every person.

MRS. CUMMING. Well, at any rate my daughters may not work for any examination or degree. You may think me a Tory, but I hold that "a lady by birth" may not condescend to sit on a school-form or soil her fingers by stitching and painting, or make them stiff by practising music.

MRS. GORDON. I really wonder you think so. Did you never read any of Miss Yonge's books?

MRS. CUMMING. Oh dear, dear! I am very much against lady authors; they do more harm than good.

MRS. GORDON. That's only a prejudice! Miss Yonge has done a great deal of good to English society in showing that work is honourable.

MRS. CUMMING. She may have shown it to others, but she would never have convinced me. I stick to my principles.

MRS. GORDON. My dear Mrs. Cumming, let me warn you, as it is my duty to do. You are not acting wisely in letting your dear girls waste the time of their youth.

MRS. CUMMING. You think of your favourite little proverb: *Wilful waste makes woeful want.*

MRS. GORDON. Indeed I do. But after all I have only to *mind my own business* and not interfere with yours. Excuse my doing so.

MRS. CUMMING. Don't apologize. I appreciate the feeling that prompts your interference; it is a kind interest in our welfare.

MRS. GORDON. I am glad you do not mind. I should only like to add: *Trust no future, howe'er pleasant.*

MRS. CUMMING. Well, as for the future, I don't trouble about it; as you say yourself, we should not *meet troubles halfway.*

MRS. GORDON. You seem to hint to me: *Practise what you preach.*

MRS. CUMMING. You have *hit the right nail on the head.* — But here are our children coming down the avenue; do not let them see what a hot discussion we have had about them; let them feel happy and comfortable. Here they are already.

SCENE III.

All the four girls come into the room in different costumes and attitudes LILY carrying some flowers, dahlias, which she means to copy, Nelly a little basket on her arm, Miss CUMMING in a boating costume and a sailor hat, Miss KATE in a bicycle costume of Oxford blue.

MRS. GORDON (getting up and shaking hands with the Misses Cumming). So you have all met. Nellie, just ring the bell; we will have tea.

(A servant with an English cap comes into the room with a tea-tray; they all sit down round a little tea-table. Mrs. Gordon pours out tea at a little side-table with Mrs. Cumming, the two ladies talk in an undertone.

ALICE. Did you act St. Elizabeth again to-day, good Nell? The Rector ought to engage you as one of his curates.

KATE. Indeed he ought to. You do just as much work as one of them.

NELLIE. I wish you would'nt always tease me. I am only doing a little.

ALICE. I am a very horrid girl; am I not, Lily?

KATE. Indeed, sometimes you are.

LILY. I don't think Kate means half the things she says. She only wishes *to rub up people the wrong way.*

KATE. Don't you think it would be awfully dull, if people were not told often, what *goes against the grain* with them? Why, they would never have an opportunity of getting into a temper and their temper might get rusty.

LILY. Please tell me if your tea is sweet enough? Will you have some of these "sweeties" Nell made?

ALICE. Nell, you made them! dear me, you little cook — how I should hate to be kitchen-maid and to be toasted and roasted.

NELLIE. You are not more toasted and roasted than on the river, for in fact you look quite sunburnt already.

KATE. Yes, we have been fishing a good deal in our punt. Won't you learn rowing, Lily?

LILY. Thank you dear, I should like to, when I have finished with the School of Art; but do you think I shall learn it easily?

ALICE. Why not? *Where there's a will, there's a way.*

NELLIE. Lily is very energetic, so she will overcome all difficulties.

LILY. But you know I am rather awkward in sports.

ALICE. Now, Lily, you are *fishing for compliments* already. You managed my bicycle very well the very first time you sat on it. Why don't you ride one yourself?

LILY. Because our dear mother does not approve of any other bodily exercise but the "Constitutional"; besides I have little time left for recreation after all the practising I have to do for my music master.

KATE. Then your "virtuoso" will be great on the piano — but what's the use of it? You need not set up as a music mistress some day, or perform in St. James' Hall.

LILY. Don't be too sure. Perhaps I may have to set up as a teacher of music and painting some day; one never knows.

NELLIE. Yes, Kate, Mother says *There's many a slip betwixt the cup and the lip.*

ALICE. Let me tell you that these little cakes are delicious. Nell, you are very domesticated; you must marry a curate.

KATE. And fill your basket with these good things and distribute them on your way through the village . . .

ALICE. And have all the little brats at your heels — I am glad mine are mostly on the pedals of my bicycle when I pass through the village.

LILY. I propose to go out into the garden to look at Nell's flower-garden, if you will not have another cup of tea.

KATE. No, thanks!

ALICE. We have quite done. Let us admire the garden of good little Nellie. She will soon be a professional gardener and not only win prizes at the shows, but sell for a good price her seeds and flowers.

NELLIE. Now, Kate, with all your teasing you have put a good idea into my head — I will indeed sell my seeds and give the profits to the Cottage Hospital.

LILY. What a good plan. I will sell one or two pictures too — that might enable us to keep up a bed.

KATE. Well, you are paragons; we tease you, as we feel dull and "ennuyées", you take it all very kindly and you even profit by it.

ALICE. I sometimes wish I had an object in life — but I couldn't possibly give up high-life and society.

NELLIE. You would not lose much by it and you would gain a good deal; *the sooner* you see it, *the better.*

KATE. *It is never too late to mend;* so for the present let us continue our old way of living and go out into the flower-garden and enjoy nature. (All the girls go out.)

MRS. GORDON. We had better have a little turn too, my dear friend, remembering: *A penny's worth of mirth is worth a pound's worth of trouble.*

—

ACT II.

SCENE I.

A little boudoir in Mrs. CUMMING's house very elegantly furnished; a beautiful hearthrug before a marble fire-place, on the mantle piece Etruscan vases with flowers and a carved "étagère". Mrs. CUMMING sitting before a little bureau of mahogany, holding carelessly a letter in her right hand, in her left a cambric pocket handkerchief.

MRS. CUMMING. My tenants already pay less rent, and now the investments bring less interest: so my agent tells me. What a shock! Mrs. Gordon always warned me, and I never believed her. I wish I had! What will become of my girls, my poor girls! How shall I break the sad news to them, poor darlings! I wish Mrs. Gordon would undertake this difficult task. How I wish she would call! *A friend in need is a friend indeed.* She may have heard of the crash, as so many suffer by it. She is my only hope now, a staunch friend in adversity. I should not like to tell the people I meet in society how I feel. Oh dear — life is indeed uncertain, "ships are but boards, and sailors men" old Shylock is right: "there be land-rats and water-rats".

I remember now all my dear friend told me. — How could I act so foolishly and never prepare my dear girls for the struggle of life. Oh dear, dear, what shall I do?

(She begins to cry.) (There is a knock at the front-door, the housemaid passes through the room to open the door, but MRS. CUMMING does not even notice her —, a minute after she announces MRS. GORDON.)

MRS. CUMMING (waking from her stupor). My dear friend, do you know the misfortune that has happened to me? I am quite bewildered, quite *at my wits' end.*

MRS. GORDON. My dear Mrs. Cumming, I hoped you were not affected in the general crash. I came to hear what your agent has written to you.

MRS. CUMMING. You may hear it all. He tells me that my investments in the railway in India are bad, that my tenants' rents cannot possibly be raised — in fact that he advises me either to let my house or to live on a very small income, and to reduce the number of my servants. I can never do that!

MRS. GORDON. But why not, my dear friend? You must not say "I cannot", but you must pray for Divine help to bear your cross and *all will come right in the end.*

MRS. CUMMING. *Man proposes and God disposes.* I wished to make life bright and smooth for my children; now their path will be rough and full of thorns.

MRS. GORDON. Remember that all may be smoothed by God's hand who overruleth all — and who can help you to get over all the difficulties of this life.

MRS. CUMMING. I heard you say before — *Man's extremity is God's opportunity,* and *After the storm comes the calm;* what a comfort it is to have you near me. Now, my very dear friend, advise me what to do.

MRS. GORDON. To begin with, *Take care of the penny, and the pound will take care of itself;* begin with reducing your number of servants. Give the kitchen-maid, your daughters' maid and the parlour-maid a month's notice — the wages of these three servants together amount to about £ 50 per annum. Let Katie help the cook, and Alice the housemaid, whilst you do the mending, and you will not feel less comfortable.

MRS. CUMMING. My poor dear girls — they have never been much indoors; they are so accustomed to out-of-door exercise.

MRS. GORDON. Never mind; they will soon take to their new duties, especially when they see that their mother feels happy to see them perform them cheerfully.

MRS. CUMMING. But what about the stable-people? I can't dismiss my old coachman . . . and I can't walk about the country like a poor person!

MRS. GORDON. You might keep the pony-trap and one pony for yourself, your girls ride the bicycle; — as for your old coachman, keep him by all means, send away the head-gardener; the coachman is a good hand at gardening. he can superintend the garden boys, — if he wants advice, Nellie will give it him quite willingly.

MRS CUMMING. Your idea is excellent; I even think my girls might like to do some gardening; they have some taste in laying out the garden beds, only they never bothered about it, so far.

MRS. GORDON. They will soon think work a pleasure and no trouble. Believe me, my dear Mrs. Cumming, *there is no law like necessity*; it very often obliges people to do a thing they dislike, and soon they find it a pleasure.

MRS. CUMMING. *Let us hope for the best and be prepared for the worst* — then we shall not be disappointed. These dear girls will often *feel at a loss*.

MRS. GORDON. My dear Mrs. Cumming, that does not matter; *a dearly bought lesson is the best* — besides my girls will be ever ready to advise and help them — so do take courage, *look at the bright side*. Your girls will not feel dull any more; they will soon feel bright and be as happy and *merry as crickets*.

MRS. CUMMING. You know how to cheer one; thank you, dear friend.

MRS. GORDON. Rather thank God who has spared the lives of your dear ones — earthly losses are nothing. "The love of money is the root of all evil" the Bible says. So far you trusted too much to your earthly possessions; now take a higher aim: the welfare of others.

MRS. CUMMING. Indeed you always seemed happier than I. I am in hopes that my dear children look upon this misfortune as an unavoidable trial.

MRS. GORDON. Which may be for their everlasting good. Therefore, dear friend, leave off grumbling and sighing, and tell them with a cheerful heart what has happened to you, and encourage them *to make the best of it*. I leave you as I hear them come.

MRS. CUMMING. A thousand thanks, my dear friend.

SCENE II.

Kate and Alice enter the room, with some tennis-balls and rackets, with Kate Greenaways aprons, as they had been playing at tennis.

KATE. We have had a famous game, have'nt we, Alice?

ALICE. Mother dear, what is the matter with you? You look all in a flurry.

MRS. CUMMING. My very dear children, just sit down and put your rackets away. I must have a little talk with you.

KATE. Mother, don't get sentimental like Mrs. Gordon, else I shall begin to laugh.

MRS. CUMMING. You may not laugh at Mrs. Gordon any more; she is the most sensible woman I ever met.

KATE. And her girls are the most sensible young women I ever met; pray excuse me, I feel quite elated and high-spirited.

MRS. CUMMING. I am glad you do, I hope you will *keep up your spirits* too after having heard my bad news.

ALICE. Oh dear mother, I hope none of our cousins are ill . . .

MRS. CUMMING. No, dear, as far as I know, they enjoy perfect health. It is a different matter altogether: a money-matter . . .

KATE. Dearest mother, I thought your agent managed your money-matters for you?

MRS. CUMMING. So he does, but in this case I shall have to manage the matter for myself. He tells me my last investments are bad. My income will be considerably reduced.

ALICE. Is that all, mother? that need not upset you so; as long as we are all well, that does not matter.

KATE. Meantime I will keep up my spirits, for *a merry heart goes all the way.*

MRS. CUMMING. I am most thankful to have such "plucky" daughters. I will tell you what my friend Mrs. Gordon advised me to do.

KATE. To send us to London and let one become short-hand-writer to an M. P., or to go to a telegraph office and become office-lady.

MRS. CUMMING. Nothing of the sort. Mrs. Gordon says: *Charity begins at home.* Keep your daughters at home; reduce the number of your domestics and let your daughters help in housekeeping.

KATE. I see — Let them put on a white apron and a cap, run and open the door when the front-door bell rings, and receive your visitors in the entrance hall.

ALICE. There, you are joking again. I know you do not mind doing anything in order to be able to stay at home. Don't believe her, mother, she often told me she would rather scrub all the floors than ever go away from you.

MRS. CUMMING. We have not quite come to that, dearest. I shall be able to keep a cook, a housemaid and a gardener.

KATE. Quite enough servants to worry one, but now I will be serious. Do not think I shall dislike doing the work of second housemaid; on the contrary, that's just what I like. I can exercise my legs by running up and down stairs, then I need not ride the bicycle every morning.

ALICE. And I shall be delighted to help in the kitchen, to be kitchenmaid and parlourmaid, dress the dishes and lay the cloth. I have long wished to know something of cookery.

MRS. CUMMING. How delighted I am! *that's an ill wind that blows no one any good.* I daresay my dear friend is .right. Mrs. Gordon says: You will feel happier for having some work to do.

ALICE. I am sure we shall, as we are able to stay at home, for *half a loaf is better than no bread.* When shall we begin?

MRS. CUMMING. I will give the servants I dismiss, a month's notice; during that time you can get to know your work *little by little.* I will tell them why I send them away.

ALICE. They will be sorry to leave.

KATE. They have had a nice time with us, half the time they have not done their work.

MRS. CUMMING. Let us see that you do yours better, then, my dear.

KATE. I know that the best china won't come to pieces in my hands.

ALICE. But you will always be *as innocent as a new born babe*, when it is broken.

MRS. CUMMING. Leave off teasing and wrangling. here comes Jane — leave me with her.

ACT III.

Mrs. CUMMING sitting in her room again, this time hemming some pocket-handkerchiefs and looking very much pleased. — Counts them:

MRS. CUMMING. There! One, two, three, four, five, six; the half dozen is hemmed, only the initials to be put in: I hear the bell, our dear friends are coming.

(Mrs. Gordon enters the room announced by Kate in a plain apron; Nellie and Lily follow with a little bag each and they shake hands. Alice comes in with a tea-tray, on which tea is served as before. Mrs. Cumming pours out, the girls pass the plates with bread and butter and little cakes.)

KATE. Now dears, all be seated; this is the first month of our service; the superfluous servants have gone and you can't think how peaceful our home is.

ALICE. Yes, Nell dear, we get quite meek and gentle — there is no need for losing our temper, everything goes as smoothly as in your house; we have all our meals quite punctually.

MRS. CUMMING. I am quite delighted with my daughters, I must say. They are far happier too, they own.

MRS. GORDON. I am so glad to hear it. I felt sure *all was wisely ordered for the best.*

KATE. Thank you so much, Mrs. Gordon, for advising my mother so kindly.

ALICE. We really feel greatly indebted to you.

MRS. GORDON. Pray don't mention it, I only advised your mother, you were ready to help to the best of your abilities, so you have done more than I.

ALICE. Try my cakes now, Nellie, three months ago I did not dream of making any.

KATE. Have some of my nice tea.

NELLIE. All is excellent; soon we shall taste home-made bread here.

ALICE. Not just yet. Do you know, Nell, I should like to come to the Sewing-Class with you some day.

KATE. And I should like to join the Women's Reform Club some day.

MRS. CUMMING. Gently, my dear, you had better ask Lily to give you some lessons in music and drawing before you join the Higher Education circle.

MRS. GORDON. I should like you to join me in answering this letter which I received this morning from your cousin, Captain Douglas.

MRS. CUMMING. Captain Douglas, why, is he ill — and does he wish any of us to come and amuse him?

MRS. GORDON (takes a letter out of her bag and reads). "Dear Mrs. Gordon, a rumour has reached me that my dear cousin Mrs. Cumming has suffered from the crash two months ago, and that she has to live on a reduced income. Why didn't she tell me of it? I have no family and I should only be too happy to add £ 500 every year to her income. Please tell me if the report is true and what I had better do. and how I can offer my help to her. My cousin has ever been a proud woman — but I cannot bear the thought that she and her dear girls are not so well off as before. With many thanks, yours truly, Robert Douglas."

KATE. Cousin Robert thinking of us! I always thought he was the most selfish of all men born and bred on earth.

MRS. CUMMING. It is good of him. I never doubted he was kind-hearted, only I never should have told him of my misfortunes.

ALICE. I think we had better tell him that we are far happier in having learnt *to put our shoulders to the wheel* and that we do not wish to accept his kind offer.

MRS. CUMMING. He would be deeply offended — but really we do not wish for the yearly contribution.

KATE. I never dreamt that the "Prince Charmant" would knock at our door.

ALICE. Or "l'oncle d'Amérique" send such a message.

MRS. CUMMING. This time I have a suggestion to make to you which Mrs. Gordon and you all will like.

ALICE. What is it? please, tell us!

MRS. CUMMING. Supposing we accepted the kind offer, for we have learned to *put our pride into our pocket* by now!

KATE. But pray, mother dear, do not let these troublesome servants come back to our house!

ALICE. Oh pray, don't! We are so happy that we are of some use in the world.

MRS. CUMMING. No, I am not wishing for their return any more than you are. I am even thinking of putting more work on your shoulders.

KATE. Then it is work and not *an old head on young shoulders.*

ALICE. Do let mother tell us her plan.

MRS. CUMMING. Well, my dears. We shall needs have to accept our generous cousin's offer, but as we are no longer selfish people we shall do some good with the money.

MRS. GORDON. How kind of you, dear Mrs. Cumming.

KATE. I know what you wish to do.

ALICE. I too — to do some good to Nell's parishioners.

MRS. CUMMING. And to ours too — supposing we supported a ward in the Infirmary with this liberal sum.

NELL. How much the poor would bless you for it!

KATE. Oh yes, do let us carry out that, mother dear!

ALICE. And not only that, but, dearest, allow us to go in for sick nursing too. You were ever averse to it formerly, let me learn it now.

MRS. CUMMING. I have changed my mind too on this point. I was afraid you might catch colds or some contagious disease.

ALICE. But now you see that I am not so apt to catch anything since I am exposed to draughts and heat, I feel much stronger.

KATE. You will *catch it* from me, if you come home with German measles.

LILY. Don't joke on so serious a subject — let her begin by nursing the old women who don't get them.

KATE. Very well, mother, give her your sanction, but allow me too to join the "Women's Reform Club for Higher Education" or at least to support it by a handsome contribution, as I feel so much interested in the work.

MRS. CUMMING. My dear Mrs. Gordon, you were right in saying *There is always a silver lining to the darkest cloud.*

Afflictions often are blessings is disguise. I thought the loss of some money was a great loss; now I see it was no loss at all, but a great gain.

KATE. It made us give up our dull way of living for amusements only.

ALICE. And take up a new way of living full of home duties.

MRS. CUMMING. And our home is a happier one since.

MRS. GORDON. And the whole village will benefit by this wonderful change. How glad Captain Douglas will be!

MRS. CUMMING. I had better answer his kind letter myself.

KATE. I will add a few lines inviting him to come and stay with us.

ALICE. I will do the cooking all by myself when he is here.

NELLIE. I will bring you my best recipes.

KATE. And I will polish the house inside and outside before he comes.

MRS. CUMMING. And now let us have a little tune from one of you.

KATE. Let us sing "Home, sweet Home", as we cannot sing anymore the "Song of the Shirt" after our new luck.

II

Anything for a Tennis-Match.

Persons.

DAISY, aged 16.   AUNT ELIZABETH.
GEORGIE, aged 14.   MISS PARKER, the governess.

SCENE I.

Daisy and Georgie are sitting in the school-room, learning some passage from Shakespeare.

DAISY (after having looked into the book very steadily). Now Georgie, hurry up. I shall soon have done.

GEORGIE. Oh dear, it is such a bore to be cramming indoors when the sun shines bright.

DAISY. Do you mean to say it is more pleasant to be doing lessons when it is pouring with rain?

GEORGIE. I mean to say it is nicest not to have to cram lessons at all.

MISS PARKER (coming into the school-room). My dear Georgie, do you think you would like learning nothing at all all day long?

GEORGIE. Indeed I should; I have plenty to do all the time without doing lessons. I have to look after the guinea-pigs and to feed the rabbits, to clean their hutch, to take the goat a little walk, to bring the ponies some bread-crusts . . .

MISS PARKER. Do stop, child! You forget that you would not enjoy all these little amusements if you had not done some work before, for "only that is hearty fun which comes after work is done".

GEORGIE. You always tell us so, but I don't believe it. I can enjoy fun without having done any work at all.

MISS PARKER. It does not matter whether you see it or not. I shan't let you leave this school-room before you can recite the passage I told you to learn. You had better set about it at once whilst I give Daisy her music-lesson in the boudoir. Be quick, I shall be back very soon.

SCENE II.

GEORGIE (alone). Aunt Elizabeth always says: "Well begun is half done." I don't see that either, but I will begin as I have to.

(She reads): "Friends, Romans, countrymen, lend me your ears" ... really what a thing to ask of them; how can they lend their ears to any body. I wish Mr. Antony had asked me. I should have said: "At your service, Sir — no, Sir, I will lend you my pen-knife, my garden-scissors, my paper-cutter, anything you like on condition that you return it to me, but I won't lend you my ears; you might forget to return them and then how queer I should look". Fancy Antony calling these old Romans his friends, he did not know them personally; he did not even know their names. Now I know all my friends and my enemies too. There is Jessie Wiley — she is my greatest friend, when she does not choose to quarrel with me. There's Kitty Hills; she is a great friend of mine too, when she does not tease my dear little pug-dog. There's Milly Walter. I like her well enough too, especially when she lets me drive her pony-cart. But I know my enemies too. There's my greatest natural enemy, Miss Parker; she keeps me indoors to learn stupid poetry when the sun is shining bright. She is really cruel to me! I hate lessons, I hate all grown-up people! I wouldn't make children learn lessons at all, especially on such a fine afternoon as this. I shall never open a book myself, when I am grown-up, I shan't have one in the house even. How I wish I were grown-up already this very day, this very hour, then I would kick all books about — there you go.

(She kicks her books about.) I shan't pick you up — let one of these old Romans do it.

(Aunt Elizabeth has been watching her for some time, she comes into the school-room now and goes up to Georgie, who does not at first notice her.)

SCENE III.

AUNT ELIZABETH. Georgie — Georgie, what are you doing?

GEORGIE (frightened). Oh dear Auntie — pray don't tell Mamma, don't tell Miss Parker; she is my natural enemy. I am quite sure she is — she treats me in quite a hostile way.

AUNT ELIZABETH. I overheard all you said, child — how can you be so unjust, how can you get such wrong ideas into your head?

GEORGIE. I don't think they are at all wrong. If you knew what she makes me learn off by heart: first Hamlet's "To be or not to be". Yes I should learn it, if it were "to be out in the sunshine and not to be in this dusky room". The Merchant of Venice: "The quality of Mercy". Nobody cares about being merciful to me! Othello's "Who steals my purse" ... they steal my time, which is more precious than any purse — Henry IV's "How many of my poorer subjects". Who can be poorer than I am, to be boxed up in this school-room? — (she begins to cry bitterly) and in conclusion, last but not least, that awfully long passage "Friends, Romans" friends whom you don't know a bit — Romans who have all been dead ever so long. I can't help hating Shakespeare for writing so much, and I don't like Miss Parker who makes me learn it.

AUNT ELIZABETH. What a shame, Georgie, to behave like this. I never knew you had such a bad temper. I had better leave you, you unruly child (she is going, Georgie clings to her).

GEORGIE. Pray don't go — I am so unhappy, Auntie, I shall cry my eyes out.

AUNT ELIZABETH. All by your own fault. If you wish me to stay here, you must first pick up these books; you must put the room straight. A young girl's school-room ought always to look like a drawing-room and be in perfect order.

(Georgie rather reluctantly picks up the books she has thrown about; she puts the books straight, but still grumbling.)

AUNT ELIZABETH. What are you grumbling at still, Georgie?

GEORGIE. Oh auntie, why must children now-a-days learn so many lessons! My friend Jessie told me that she heard a medical man (doctor) say: it is very bad for girls to be so much indoors — she says besides, our grandmothers did not learn half we have to learn, and they were very happy all the same.

AUNT ELIZABETH. Your friend Jessie thinks herself very wise — she forgot to tell you that times are altogether different. Your grand-mothers travelled in coaches; they very seldom travelled abroad, so they had no need to study foreign languages, when they were young. In their numerous spare moments they did some fancy-work, quietly sitting at home in their family circle. And they never wasted their time in playing croquet or lawn-tennis.

GEORGIE. Never played tennis? Oh poor dears! now I don't envy them any longer, I begin to pity them. What a privation that would be for me never to play tennis.

AUNT ELIZABETH. But you do not deserve to be allowed to play tennis, if you do not do your work cheerfully. You shall not play for another week.

GEORGIE. Oh auntie dear, don't say so, I must play. I must beat Jessie in the next match; she beat me last time, and I can't bear being beaten.

AUNT ELIZABETH. Very well, Georgie. Unless you learn Antony's address to the Romans very well indeed at once, you shall certainly not play tennis this week. I shall tell your mother how you behaved, and you shall see what you will play at for the present. I guess, at keeping indoors all day long and at going to bed at 7 o'clock every night.

GEORGIE. Pray, auntie dear, don't tell any one how I behaved. I will be well behaved now. I promise you. I won't kick my books about the room any more. I won't call Miss Parker my natural enemy again (altho' she is). I won't do anything naughty. I really won't.

AUNT ELIZABETH. I shall believe you when I see you do what you promise. I leave you now, but I will look in again before I call on some friends. I will see if you can recite your "Oration" well. (She leaves the room).

GEORGIE. Dear, dear! not any tennis this week — that can't be. I will do anything for a tennis-match. I'll certainly learn this old speech. Now, friends, Romans, countrymen, do come, and countrywomen too. I will lend you both my ears even if you should pull them. I don't care any more. I had rather have both my ears pulled than miss the tennis-match this week and let Jessie say she beat me. I am good now. How very much surprised Miss Parker will be when she comes up — she will think me quite tame and will wonder at this great change.

SCENE IV.

Miss PARKER comes into the room without Daisy whom she has sent into the garden. She finds GEORGIE poring over her book; she stands at a distance and looks at her, saying to herself:

"I am surprised! What a change — so her fit of temper is over — a very strange girl, this Georgie."

MISS PARKER (aloud). Do you know your passage now — at least the part I told you to learn for to-day?

GEORGIE (quite meekly). I think I do. Miss Parker — please let me say it. — (She stands up and says it quite correctly to the great surprise of her governess.)

MISS PARKER. I am quite surprised, Georgie. You see now how easily you can retain poetry, if you only set about it. Why did you not learn your passage before?

GEORGIE. Because — because I didn't choose to.

MISS PARKER. What a very rude answer — why did you choose to learn your poetry now, if I may ask?

GEORGIE. Because — because — unless I had chosen to learn it, I should not have been allowed to play at the tennis-match this week.

MISS PARKER. I see, I see. Your mother has been here and found you out.

GEORGIE. Please, Miss Parker, it was not mother, who was here, it was aunt Elizabeth.

MISS PARKER. All the better, then she saw what an ill-tempered child you are.

GEORGIE. But please, Miss Parker, I will not be ill-tempered any more — (aside) at any rate not before the tennis-match is over. I promise you.

MISS PARKER. What makes you promise that?

GEORGIE. If I am not sweet-tempered, aunt Elizabeth will prevent my beating Jessie in our great tennis-match.

MISS PARKER. I see, I see again. Your sharp aunt has found out your vulnerable point.

GEORGIE. I am sorry to say she has found out all — she overheard my ejaculations (outbursts of temper) — and so she has not only found me out, but I have found out too, that it is nicer to learn one's lessons without grumbling, because grown-up people will force children to learn them.

MISS PARKER. If we did not see the necessity of it, we should not force little people to learn them; unless you learn lessons when you are young, you will be a dunce when you are old.

GEORGIE. I should not exactly like to be a dunce, but above all I should like just now to beat all these friends, Romans and countrymen at the tennis-match, for I am no more afraid of them.

The curtain falls.

III.

A Telegram.

Persons.

LADY ELGIN.   ANNIE, the ladies maid.
Miss ELGIN (Maud).   JANE, the housemaid.
Miss MABEL ELGIN.   MRS. EASTON, the cook.

SCENE I.

Lady ELGIN is sitting in her room, writing some letters, when her
daughter MAUD hurries in, calling:

Mamma, cook has just got a telegram — the housemaid
told me the postman ran from the post-office down the avenue
to deliver it, as it has "urgent" on it. But, poor thing, she
won't open it; she screams and shrieks with fright, she says
she never received a telegram before in her life. She cries
out, she wishes there were no such things as telegrams —
she has even wished there were no wires in the world, so that
people could not wire.

MABEL (rushing into the room). Oh mother, you never saw
such a commotion as there is down-stairs; the ladies maid
came up all in a flurry, saying that cook simply shrieks; she
has just received a telegram and she says she won't open it,
she feels sure that her nephew who is out in Africa has been
killed by the Zulus, or perhaps that her cousin who is a
sailor has been eaten up by the savages of the Fiji-Islands
— or that her niece, the lady's maid, had been blown up
in London by the dynamitards or it may be her uncle

9*

out in India has been stung by a serpent; — but here comes Annie.

ANNIE. Please, Milady, cook is mad with grief — she has just received a telegram, and now she supposes all kinds of dreadful things have happened to her people — we all fear she will cry her eyes out.

LADY ELGIN. What nonsense! Bring me the fatal telegram. There may be very good news in it — if the news were bad, I should break it to her.

ANNIE. I am afraid, Mylady, she won't give me the telegram — she holds it tight in her hand. She won't part with it.

LADY ELGIN. Tell her I want to speak to her, bring her up here.

ANNIE. I will try to, but I fear I shan't succeed. I never saw any one in such a state except my former mistress who used to have fits of passion.

MAUD. Poor old Mrs. Easton.

(Annie goes down, the two girls sit down in easy chairs, each taking up a book.)

SCENE II.

The cook comes upstairs crying bitterly supported by Annie, the ladies maid, and Jane, the housemaid; she holds the telegram tight in her hand, and shrieks:

MRS. EASTON. (The cook.) Mylady, my whole family are either ruined or dead, else they would not have sent me such a horrid telegram; why didn't they write to me to prepare me for the shock? My heart will break, simply break, oh dear! (She begins to sob convulsively.)

LADY ELGIN. Now, Mrs. Easton, do try and be calm, you may be quite mistaken; there may be a piece of good news in this little piece of paper. Your nephew out in Africa may have been promoted, your sailor cousin may have discovered a gold-mine, your niece may have made a good match, your uncle in India may be coming home, so you had better open the telegram and see which of the good things I am supposing has come to pass.

MRS. EASTON. Dear, kind Madam! How I wish you were right, but I cannot quite believe it, as they put "wire back". — A piece of good news is always acceptable, you would wire back your good wishes with pleasure, you would not fail to do so, you need not be told to wire back. So it must necessarily be some piece of bad news. (She begins to shriek again and to sob aloud.)

LADY ELGIN. Do compose yourself! I feel sure you are worrying about nothing. Open the telegram now.

MRS. EASTON. I should like to know what is in it, but I can't open it myself. I really can't, I have no strength to open it.

LADY ELGIN. If you will allow me, I will open it. I will not tell you what's in it, unless it be some good news. Let us hope sincerely that the telegram contains some very good piece of news.

MRS. EASTON. You will be greatly disappointed. If you have the courage to open it, here it is, Mylady, but pray do not tell me all the dreadful things contained in it.
(Lady Elgin opens the telegram very slowly; she begins to laugh when she reads it.)

LADY ELGIN. I never heard of such fun! No wonder they put "wire back", there's not a minute to be lost.

MRS. EASTON. What a comfort! Mylady laughs, so there must be a piece of good news after all.

LADY ELGIN (beginning to read). "Left a band-box in your room, with a new bonnet for Mrs. Montgomery to wear at the wedding of her son at 12 o'clock; wire back to say if you can send it to her at once, or else I shall have to send her another."
(General hilarity.)

MRS. EASTON (quite relieved). Is that all? a band-box left in my room with only a bonnet in it — well, I never, fancy sending a telegram for a stupid bonnet! I shall give that young milliner a piece of my mind when I wire back, about waste and stupidity and forgetfulness and frightening people out of their wits, and I don't know what.

LADY ELGIN. You see, Mrs. Easton, I was right. Now tell me if that precious band-box was really left with you, so that I can send orders to the stables to have a horse saddled for some one to ride over to Mrs. Montgomery's with the box.

MRS. EASTON. Yes it was indeed, but I should like to box that young woman's ears, who is so utterly careless, and I shall never let her enter my room again — even if her bonnets all come from Paris and are the newest fashion.

LADY ELGIN. You see, Mrs. Easton, that all your excitement was useless; another time, don't "cross the bridge before you come to it"!

The End.

—•◆•—   — —

Druck von Velhagen & Klasing in Bielefeld.